Fight for Blood

Blood Origin Series

Book 2

Tiffany Heiser

Willow Moon Publishing

Copyright © 2020 by Tiffany Heiser Published by Willow Moon Publishing 108 Saint Thomas Road Lancaster, PA 17601 willow-moon-publishing.com

Cataloging Data Heiser, Tiffany (1984-) Fight for Blood/Tiffany Heiser–

1st U.S. Edition

Summary: Rena's world takes a turn into the supernatural when she finds out Cryder is not human and is destined to be with her. His destiny is irrevocably linked to Rena's. She's forced to jump into this supernatural world without the time to consider the possibilities of this new world with vampires, because it looks like Cryder has brought more than his mysterious demeanor, but a rogue vampire hell-bent on taking her blood for his own. There's nowhere to run, so Rena must learn to fight back and become the true person she was meant to be.

122 pages; 216 x 140 mm Hardcover ISBN-13:9781948256315
1.YoungAdult/Fiction/Romance/Paranormal.2.YoungAdult/Fiction/Roman ce/Vampires 3. Young Adult/Fiction/Romance/General Yearn for Blood. Heiser, Tiffany Printed in the United States on acid free paper Typeset: Sabon NextLT Edited by Kat Helgeson Design by Jodi Stapler

I'd love to dedicate this to my family and friends who have pushed me forward, and reminded me that I could do anything that I put my mind to

ACKNOWLEDGEMENTS

I'd like to thank my family and friends, those that took time to read what I wrote and to continue to push me. For those that have been walking with me through the process and stayed on the phone to listen to ideas, or long-winded ramblings; I adore and appreciate each one of you and give my many thanks for the support and love.

CONTENTS

Chapter One

"Rena! Hey, Rena! Smile!"

I pivoted on the spot and faced my best friend Cecile's mother. Mrs. Danvers held up a camera and took a picture of me. I had to struggle to hoist a smile onto my face, but I managed, barely.

This should have been one of the happiest days of my life. I'd graduated high school, after all, something I'd spent most of the last few years looking forward to leaving behind me.

But that was when I thought high school would be followed by the usual things. The normal things. College. Finding a job. Getting an apartment on my own. Things I could look forward to in an easy, uncomplicated way. I knew now that the life that awaited me, the life I would be embarking upon this very night, would be the most complex thing I'd ever experienced.

Mrs. Danvers looked at the picture on her camera's display. "This is a good one," she said enthusiastically. "I'm going to frame it and put it on the mantelpiece."

The smile on my face was genuine this time. "I'm really going to miss you," I told her.

"Are you sure you girls want to do this backpacking through Europe thing?" Mrs. Danvers asked.

I hated this conversation. She kept asking, and I knew that

even though she was mostly joking, there was a part of her that longed for me to say no; to renounce our summer trip and stay home.

I was lucky to have her. I knew that. Mrs. Danvers was the closest thing I had to a mother. She'd raised me, let me live in her home, ever since the car accident that had taken away my own parents. It was thanks to her that I had someone here at my graduation at all.

Well, someone other than Cryder, that was.

He appeared at my elbow, materializing as if from nowhere the way he always seemed to. "Congratulations," he said, and Mrs. Danvers raised her camera again and took a photo of the two of us together.

I swatted at my boyfriend's arm. "What have I said about this?" I asked. "You can't just creep up on people. Make a noise or something. Let me know you're behind me."

He grinned and pulled me into an embrace. "It's not my fault you weren't listening."

"You've gotten better at acting human," I told him. "But you've still got a long way to go."

"Well, we can set my human lessons aside for the moment," Cryder said. "It's time for you to learn how to assimilate into *my* culture."

My nerves sparked again.

I'd known it was coming, of course. I'd known for weeks now, ever since I'd met Cryder and he'd told me about my family's history and my own strange nature.

"Are you sure we have to do this?" I asked him. "We couldn't just...just stay here?"

"You know we can't," he said. "And we agreed on this. We agreed that it was the best course of action."

"Cecile's mom thinks we're just going away for the summer," I said. "What are we going to tell her? How are we going to explain why we're not coming back?"

"We'll figure something out," he said, resting a hand on my lower back.

9

"Is it even possible that we might come back here someday?"

"Anything's possible," Cryder said. "You never can tell."

***

Drake was waiting for us back at the house. He gave me a quick hug when we got out of the car and then took Cecile in his arms. Cryder looked away politely as they kissed, but I didn't. It did me good to see my best friend get a little action.

"Do you kids have to go right to the airport?" Mrs. Danvers asked. "Couldn't you come in for some coffee cake?"

"Sorry, Mrs. Danvers," Drake said. "We need to leave now if we're going to make it through international security in time to catch our flight to Rome."

"Oh...well, all right," she agreed, wringing her hands. "Call me when you land, won't you?"

"Of course, Mom." Cecile hugged her mother. "And remember, you can track the flight online, so you'll be able to see where we are the whole time. Do you still have the website I showed you pulled up on the computer?"

"I've got it," Mrs. Danvers said. "You're sure you want to do this?"

"Definitely," Cecile said.

"Don't worry, Mrs. Danvers," I added. "Cryder has family in Rome. They'll be meeting us at the airport, and we'll be staying with them for a while. So, it's not like we'll be alone."

"All right," Mrs. Danvers agreed. "You kids be safe." She hugged Cryder and Drake, each of whom responded somewhat awkwardly. Neither of them seemed to have mastered the subtle difference between the romantic hug and the hug of motherly affection, and they dealt with their confusion by standing stiff as boards and waiting for the event to be over.

We loaded our luggage into the back of Drake's car, which we would be abandoning at the airport. This was the part of the plan I found stupid—surely it would have been easier to find someone to give us a ride? But Drake had insisted. He loved driving in America, he said. It was so different from driving in Rome, and he was determined to soak up every last bit of it.

Then, all too soon, we were driving away, leaving our home behind us.

Cecile and I knelt in the backseat, our noses pressed to the rear window, watching her mother. Mrs. Danvers was standing at the end of her driveway and waving to us. "Do you think we'll ever see her again?" Cecile asked, swallowing as her voice hitched.

"Definitely," I said. I felt guilty about the fact that Cecile had gotten caught up in this. It hadn't been my fault, exactly, but it couldn't be denied that if she hadn't been my friend, none of this would be happening to her. She would be off to college, like everyone else in our class.

"We'll come back for a visit someday," Drake said.

Cryder cleared his throat, and I could tell he was trying to discourage Drake from overpromising. Because the truth was, who could say whether we ever would?

Who could say whether it would ever be safe for two vampires of royal blood to be around humans?

The attack on Cecile—the attack that had been because of me—had come from a vampire who thirsted for my potent royal blood. Because of that attack, Cecile had been turned. She had lost her very humanity thanks to her friendship with me.

I couldn't risk that happening to Mrs. Danvers, or to anyone else I loved.

Leaving was next to impossible. But coming back was likely to be even harder. I knew I would have to stay away.

***

"Are you nervous?" Cryder asked.

"Of course, I'm nervous," I said. The two of us had found seats at the gate from which our plane would be departing. Now I lowered my voice so that none of the people sitting nearby would hear. "I've only met three vampires in my life. You, Drake, and—" I shuddered. "Bristol."

"No one in my family is like Bristol," Cryder assured me. "They're excited to meet you, not to *eat* you."

"I mean, I know that," I said. "But you did say the ritual I would have to go through would be painful."

Cryder hesitated. "Best not to think about that until we arrive," he said. "There's no reason to overburden yourself."

"I wish you would tell me what I was going to have to do," I said. It was hard flying to Rome with absolutely no idea of what I was getting myself into.

"Is there anything I could tell you that would make you change your mind?" he asked.

I knew it was a sincere question, so I gave it the consideration it deserved. "No," I said finally. "I want to be with you." I was a little frightened by how badly I wanted to be with Cryder. I had never had serious feelings for a guy before him. To go from that, to wanting to devote my eternal soul to somebody, was disconcerting to say the least.

And then there was the idea of being a part of the royal family. By marrying Cryder, I would become queen to his king. I had no idea what that was going to entail, and it was a frightening thought. Would I have to rule? I had no idea how to even begin to do that.

But if I stayed here, if I declined Cryder's offer to go to Rome...well, then *more* like Bristol were going to come. And soon.

Bristol. The violent and terrifying vampire who had pursued me for weeks, thirsted for my blood, who had turned my best friend, just because she was unlucky enough to be in his way.

The loudspeaker crackled to life. "Flight 472 to Rome, Italy is now boarding," the attendant said.

Cryder got to his feet, pulling me along with him. Even though we had been together for months now, his strength never ceased to amaze me. It was a quality he said I would have myself someday, but for now my muscles remained small and human. The quantities of vampire venom I drank on a regular basis didn't do much more than prevent me from atrophying completely.

Cecile came scampering over, a stack of magazines and a sudoku book in her hand. "Did you hear? We're boarding. It's time to go!"

I had to laugh. Cecile never let anything get her down. Even when she'd learned that she'd been bitten; that she was a part of the vampire world forever, she had adjusted to the idea remarkably quickly. I was constantly impressed by my friend.

And I was thoroughly grateful for the fact that I'd have her with me in the coming days. At least there would be something familiar. Something from home.

We got in line, dragging our carry-on luggage behind us, and headed up the jetway that led to the plane. I kept one hand firmly on my passport. I'd never left the country before, and I was terrified that something would go wrong.

Although, considering all the strange and frightening things that were waiting for me when I landed in Rome, losing my passport should have been the least of my worries.

Cryder led me to our seats in the front of the plane. He'd been able to afford first class, probably because of his family's wealth. I had never exactly come out and asked Cryder how much money he had, but I knew that as a member of the royal family it had to be a lot. So, that was one more thing I would have to adjust to. I'd never been *poor*, but the Danvers family was solidly middle-class. That was the only life I knew.

The flight attendant brought us drinks. It was strange to see Cryder doing something as basic and human as sipping a cola. I was used to seeing him try to blend in with my human friends—it was a necessary part of spending time together while I was still in school—but neither he nor Drake had really gotten the hang of it. Everything they did was always deliberate, not as if they were really human but as if they were playing human beings in a movie or something.

Before long, I'd probably be like that myself. I'd have forgotten everything that came naturally to me now about being a human girl and blending in as a part of the human world. I would be a vampire, through and through.

But this was the choice I'd made. I had decided to embrace my vampire side and to pursue this new life. I had to go all in.

I closed my eyes and steeled myself as the plane's engines roared to life.

There was no turning back now.

Chapter Two

I hadn't expected to sleep on the plane. But I hadn't anticipated how comfortable our first-class seats would be. A couple of hours into the flight, an attendant came by and helped me recline mine, transforming it into a bed. She even made it up with a blanket and pillow for me. It wouldn't be the most comfortable bed I'd ever slept in in my life, but it was a lot nicer than anything I'd expected on a flight.

I awoke several hours later to find Cryder kneeling beside me, his hand on my shoulder, his dark hair messier than usual. I knew he didn't sleep, but he must have been lying in his little bed so as not to arouse suspicion or draw attention. I reached out to comb his hair back into place with my fingers.

He smiled. "We'll be landing soon," he said. "I thought you'd like to see Rome from the air."

I did want to see that. I sat up and looked out my window. "It's only clouds," I complained.

He smiled. "You'll see more as we come down. The flight attendant is coming to turn your bed back into a seat and to give you a snack for breakfast." Then he was gone, as if he hadn't been there. I shook my head. He moved so quickly sometimes! People were going to notice that if he wasn't careful.

The flight attendant was at my side. I got out of bed so that she could rearrange my space back into a seat. When I was sitting and buckled in, she handed me a cup of juice with a foil lid and a packet of granola. I hadn't eaten much of the dinner service last night—I'd been too nervous about what lay ahead—and I found that I was extremely hungry now. I tore into my granola with gusto.

About fifteen minutes later, the plane started to descend. I pressed my nose to the window, taking in the sight of Rome from the air. The buildings were shaped so differently from what I was used to back home. How was I going to adjust to life here in Italy? I had no idea, but I was looking forward to seeing what was ahead.

The plane landed. I gathered my things and disembarked, joining Cryder, Cecile, and Drake in the terminal. Cecile was yawning and leaning on Drake's shoulder.

"We'd better go get our luggage," Cryder said. "The car will be waiting for us."

Nerves gripped me again. It was strange to think that anyone was waiting for me in Rome. I knew who the car must have been sent by—the vampire community. The royal family. They knew I was coming. They were anticipating my arrival.

I knew that the vampires were my people, that my mother had been one of them. But I had been raised all-human. I hadn't even known vampires were real until I'd met Cryder and Drake. I hadn't yet adjusted to the idea that I belonged in that world.

And not all of them were friendly. Alright, so Cryder's family wouldn't be like Bristol. I believed that. But that didn't mean no vampires would be. If I was to be their ruler, I'd eventually have to meet many of them, wouldn't I? Wouldn't I be in danger?

My thoughts were occupied with worries as I collected my suitcase from the baggage carousel and made my way outside with Cryder leading the way.

There were plenty of cars parked outside, but Cryder seemed to know immediately which one was for us. He led the way to a parked limousine. The driver stood on the sidewalk holding a sign which read *La Oscurità*.

"What's La Oscurità?" I asked as we climbed in, leaving our bags on the sidewalk for the driver to load into the trunk.

"It's Italian," Cryder said. "It means 'the darkness.'"

Well, that was terrifying. We were driving into *the darkness*?

Drake must have seen the expression on my face. "It's the name of the city where the vampire community lives," he explained. "Humans recognize it as a little township on the outskirts of Rome."

"Humans know about it?" I was stunned. "I thought it was going to be a hidden place. A secret place."

"Like an underground cave or something?" Cryder smiled.

I felt silly now. I'd been going about my normal life with Cryder at my side for months now. I knew he didn't have the lifestyle of a bat. But yes, an underground cave was something I'd imagined.

Cecile looked puzzled too. "I don't get it," she said. "You can't just have a vampire town that humans know about, can you?"

"Well, they don't know it's us living there," Cryder said.

"But wouldn't they be passing through all the time?" Cecile asked. "I thought we were going to a place where vampires lived in isolation."

"La Oscurità is like that," Drake said. "Humans know it exists, but they don't come in very often. Tourists are permitted, and sometimes they do come through. The town is a novelty to them."

"But how do you keep humans from just moving in?" I asked.

"They don't want to," Drake said. "The area repels them."

"Wouldn't it have the opposite effect? I'd think a huge concentration of vampires like you're talking about would attract humans."

The two vampires exchanged glances. "The truth is that humans generally don't feel any interest in the place," Cryder said. "It's under a spell, and the spell diverts their attention. The loophole is tourism—if a human is thinking about travel, it's possible for their thoughts to wander to La Oscurità and for them to develop an interest in spending a weekend there. But if they're thinking about a place to buy a home or to set up a business, La Oscurità repels them. Often, humans who come home from a vacation there have to explain to their friends why in the world they wanted to go to La Oscurità in the first place."

"La Oscurità is under a spell?" I repeated. "Vampires can do magic?"

"No, we can't," Cryder said. "The spell was put in place by a witch."

"A witch!" I sat back in my seat. Cecile's jaw dropped. "Witches are real?"

"This one is," Drake said with a smile. "Don't worry, she's nothing you need to worry about. She's a decent person."

"But if there are good ones, there are also bad ones, right?" I was thinking of Bristol and how he compared to the vampires sitting next to me.

"There are good and bad members of every group," Cryder agreed. He seemed to have followed my thoughts. "There are good and bad humans. There are good and bad vampires. There are good and bad witches. All you can do is take care to surround yourself with the good ones."

"And you'll be completely safe in the castle, with the royal family," Drake said. "It's one of the safest places a person could be, as long as they're under our protection. That's part of the reason we were so anxious to bring you here, Rena. Your life was in danger at home. Here, we can protect you."

The limousine pulled away from the curb. I clung to the door handle as the driver merged into traffic. The road was full of little motorbikes, cutting in between cars, speeding their way to their destinations. "Is there some kind of biker event going on?" I asked.

Cryder laughed. "That's just Rome," he said. "It's always like this. The roads in the United States are actually very organized by comparison."

He wasn't kidding. I couldn't even figure out what the lanes of traffic were—or if lanes even existed. Everyone was moving in a cluster. I'd never be able to drive here, I thought despairingly. I would be dependent on my new vampire family anytime I wanted to go somewhere. That was an unpleasant thought.

"Look out there," Cryder said. "You'll be able to see the Colosseum in a minute."

Cecile and I looked. A moment later the limo rounded a

corner and, sure enough, the familiar round stone structure came into view. I'd seen the Colosseum dozens of times in pictures and movies, but now it was right here in front of me. That was hard to believe. "Wow. That's really it?"

"That's really it," Cryder said. "Maybe we'll be able to arrange a tour of the city someday and you can see all the sights. The Pantheon, Trevi Fountain...there's a lot to see in Rome."

"Maybe," Drake said. A look passed between the two of them, and I got the feeling that Drake was reminding his cousin of something.

I sat back in my seat, trying to appreciate where I was. *Rome.* Whatever lay ahead for us, I'd made the trip to Italy. It was a journey I probably never would have taken if Cryder hadn't come into my life. Now I would have the chance to see things other people could only dream of. I'd already gotten to see the Colosseum, and my adventure was only just beginning.

The buildings thinned around us and gave way to countryside. We'd left the city. Now I looked out on fields of crops I didn't recognize. One patch of land even held young trees. I wondered what they were growing.

"Okay," Drake said. "We're about to enter the walls of La Oscurità. You two will be able to feel the effects of the spell."

"What's it going to feel like?" Cecile sounded nervous.

Drake put an arm around her. "I don't know exactly," he admitted. "I've never felt it myself. But it shouldn't be painful."

"It shouldn't be?"

"It won't be," Cryder said.

I was nervous, too. I scooted closer to him and assessed myself, trying to locate any unusual thoughts or sensations. Nothing seemed amiss.

The car slowed slightly.

"Are we stopping?" Cecile asked.

"Not stopping," Cryder said. "We need to slow down a bit to enter the town, that's all."

"I wish we'd seen more of Rome," she said.

I was feeling the same way. "We never even got to get out of the car," I complained.

"We'll try to go back another day," Cryder said.

"But what if we can't? I can't come all the way to Italy and not see anything cool. I'd like to try riding one of those scooters." Where had that thought come from? The scooters had scared me when I'd seen them. I knew that. Why did they suddenly seem so appealing?

"I thought we'd get to try some Italian food," Cecile said.

"They have food in La Oscurità," Drake told her.

"I'm sure it's not as good as what they have in Rome," she countered.

Cryder laughed. "Spell's still working, I see."

"What?" Cecile asked him.

"You want to go back to Rome because the spell is pushing you away from entering La Oscurità. That's what you're feeling. Give it a moment and it will pass."

Was that true? He was right that I did badly want to go back to Rome. But wasn't that to be expected? I'd never been to Rome. Rome was interesting. This place, this little village of La Oscurità, was boring. There was nothing here to keep our interest. Of course, we wanted to go back.

And then we were beyond the walls and the feeling disappeared as if it had never been.

Cecile gasped. I looked around in wonder. I had expected a small town, a village with cottages and peddlers selling produce from carts on the sidewalk. I had expected to feel as if I'd been transported back in time. And I *did* feel as if I'd jumped to another period in history, but in every other way, La Oscurità confounded my expectations.

The architecture was beautiful. The buildings seemed to be spun out of glass. They sat low to the ground, lower than the wall, but they were arranged beautifully around well-manicured lawns and flower gardens.

"There's the castle," Cryder said, pointing.

The castle appeared to be carved out of ebony. It rose several stories higher than the surrounding buildings, and it was beautiful. I stared out the window as we approached, drinking it in. So, this was to be my new home.

The limousine pulled between two wrought iron gates that had been thrown open. "Can anyone just walk through those gates?" I asked nervously. "I thought security would be tighter here."

"Everyone who lives in La Oscurità is loyal to the royal family," Cryder said. "You won't find any rogues like Bristol here. We have wards up against them."

"More witchcraft?" Cecile asked. I thought I heard a note of eagerness in her voice.

Drake laughed. "You're interested in witchcraft?"

"Sure, I am," Cecile said. "Who wouldn't want to be able to do magic?"

"You just became a vampire," he pointed out. "Why not focus on one thing at a time?"

"Because I'm an overachiever. You were at my graduation. I received honors!"

Drake laughed. "That's what I like about you. Always looking to the next thing."

"She'll definitely make things interesting at home," Cryder agreed wryly.

"Interesting how?" I asked.

"We've got a lot of traditions, let's just put it that way," Cryder said. "We, vampires, are set in our ways. It's not often we bring new people into the palace, especially people like you. People who are so young, both in years and in experience."

"I hope we don't make fools of ourselves," I said, feeling nervous.

Cryder wrapped an arm around me. "You won't," he said. "My parents will love you."

I had to laugh at that.

"What's funny?" he asked.

"Just, you know, meeting the parents. I know you're traditional, but really, it's such a human thing to do. Everything else about this has been so strange and unexpected but meeting my boyfriend's parents is something I always kind of expected to have to do at some point in my life."

"And that's funny?"

"What's funny is that right now I'm more afraid of that than I am of anything else!"

"My parents aren't frightening," he chuckled. "They're not going to hurt you, Rena."

"I'm not afraid they're going to hurt me. I'm afraid they won't like me. What if they don't think I'm a good fit for you? What if they don't think I belong in the royal family?"

"Don't borrow trouble," Cecile warned. "You always do this. But everyone likes you, Rena."

"Everyone doesn't like me. What are you talking about?"

"Nobody *dis*likes you. And Cryder loves you. Right?" She glanced at him.

He smiled. "Very much."

"So, his parents will like you too. Ipso facto."

Drake looked impressed. "I didn't know you spoke Latin."

"Non sequitur."

Drake laughed.

The car pulled to a halt. Through the tinted windows, I could just make out the palace doors opening and two figures emerging.

I drew in a deep, steadying breath.

Cryder took my hand and gave it a squeeze. "Let's go."

Chapter Three

I clung to Cryder's arm as we crossed the courtyard and approached the front steps of the palace. Now, that we had left the car, I could see his mother and father much more clearly.

I was amazed. They looked so young! Hardly older than Cryder himself! Of course, that probably made sense, I thought. I knew that Cryder's true age wasn't exactly reflected in his physical appearance. He was a lot older than he looked. And by that same token, his parents were probably much older too.

Still, in my head I had prepared myself for something else. I wasn't sure exactly what, but *something*. I supposed I had thought I'd be meeting people who looked more like my idea of parents. More like Cecile's mom, with her greying hair and lined face. More exhausted by the trials of life. More like they were actually ready to step away from the pressures of ruling a vampire kingdom.

They looked nothing like Cecile's mother.

Cryder's father looked more like Cryder himself than anything else. He was tall, with dark eyes and dark hair. He looked as if he was in outstanding physical shape, and it suddenly occurred to me to wonder whether vampires needed to exercise.

Cryder's mother had his bright blue eyes, but there the similarities ended. She was short of stature, with beautiful pale skin, and was dressed in a flowing gown with her hair pinned up in an elaborate style. I felt suddenly stupid in my travel sweats. Why hadn't I made a plan to change my clothes before meeting the king and queen? I was such an idiot.

These people didn't look like they were about to retire. I tried not to stare, but I couldn't help it. Cryder's mother was especially intimidating. She was the queen now, but I was going to take her place. Would she resent me?

She broke into a smile and strode forward to embrace her son. "Welcome home," she said. "You've been missed in your absence."

"Mother." He hugged her.

She turned to Drake. "Nephew. Your parents wanted to be here as well, but they were called away."

He nodded. "They must attend to their duties. I understand."

Everyone was so formal here! Would I be expected to speak that way as well? I knew I'd never be able to make it sound natural. What if I never fit in among the older vampires?

Cryder took my hand and pulled me forward. "Mother," he said, "this is Rena. My bride to be."

She took my hand in both of hers. "Rena. You're most welcome. I can't tell you how delighted we are to meet you at last."

"It's really nice to meet you too," I managed. Then I remembered my courtesies. "Your Majesty."

"My name is Giorgia," she said. "I'm only a Majesty to my subjects. You're a member of our family."

I didn't respond. Could I really call the queen of the vampires by her first name? It seemed so personal.

She looked up at Cryder. "Is she frightened?" she asked in a stage whisper. I felt myself go red with embarrassment.

"Of course, she's frightened," Cryder said. "Wouldn't you be?"

"I'm sorry, Rena," Giorgia said. "I don't often interact with...people like you."

Did she mean humans? Teenagers? Americans? "That's all right," I said.

"This is Cecile," Cryder said. "I wrote you about her."

"Ah, the human you turned," Giorgia said to Drake. "This one doesn't look frightened of me."

"Should I be?" Cecile asked, a bit more sass in her voice than I thought advisable.

Giorgia laughed. "Of course, you shouldn't," she said. "You're part of the family now, too. Samuele, come and meet Rena and Cecile."

The vampire I took to be Cryder's father glided over as if he were on oiled casters. "It's very nice to meet you both," he rumbled. "We've anticipated your arrival for quite some time."

"We should let Rena get to bed," Cryder said. "She's had a long journey, and she's tired."

Giorgia's smile faded slightly. "We can't send anyone to their quarters just yet," she said.

"Why not?" Cryder asked. "We came all the way from the States, Mother.

"I know that," Giorgia said. "But there's the ceremony to think of, Cryder. Everyone has been awaiting your arrival." She raised her voice ever so slightly. "Show them in, please."

Cryder's hand tightened on my arm. "She isn't prepared for this," he said in a low, furious voice. "She wasn't expecting it. It's unfair to spring it on her."

My heart fluttered anxiously in my chest. What was being sprung on me? What was the *ceremony*? I remembered what Cryder had told me about the trials I would have to undergo as I joined the royal family. They would be painful, he'd said. Was that what was happening right now? He was right; I wasn't ready!

The courtyard surrounding the entrance to the palace was filling up with people. *No,* I reminded myself, *not people.* These were vampires. We were still in the town of La Oscurità, after all, right in the heart of it. And this was a place that repelled humans and welcomed vampires, so the newcomers clustered around me couldn't be anything else.

I pressed back against Cryder, terrified. Would they bite me? What were they here to do?

It was astonishing just how many of them managed to crowd their way into the courtyard. I wondered, in the back of my mind, the part of me that wasn't panicking, whether this was something that happened often. Did the king and queen regularly open their doors to their subjects in this way, allowing them onto the palace grounds? If they did, it was no wonder everyone in La Oscurità was so loyal to the crown.

"What's happening?" Cecile whispered.

"The townspeople are here to see their new rulers and to declare their allegiance as the power shifts from my parents to me and Rena," Cryder said quietly. "It's an important part of any shift in power. As rulers, we're only as strong as we are supported by our people. It's important that they know how much we value their approval, and it's important for us to know we have it."

I found my voice. "That's all it is? They're just going to tell us if they approve or not?"

He looked down at me, his hands firm and reassuring on my shoulders. "What did you think was about to happen?"

"I didn't know…"

"Oh, honey." He wrapped his arms around me. "You're overwhelmed, aren't you?"

I nodded.

"You're alright," he said quietly. "There's nothing to be afraid of. You don't have to do anything right now. They just want to see you, that's all."

"But I'm a mess. I just got off a plane. My clothes are crappy, my hair is a disaster—"

"That's the kind of thing humans notice," Cryder said. "That's not what they'll be looking for."

"What will they be looking for?"

He hesitated. "Maybe you shouldn't worry about that right now," he suggested.

"No," I said. "I want you to tell me. If you don't, I'll just imagine it's something worse than it really is."

He sighed. "Okay," he said. "Well, part of it is your bearing. The way you carry yourself. They want to believe their rulers are proud and confident."

"I'm not feeling very proud and confident."

"I know. It's okay. A lot of what you need right now, you have naturally. It's in your bloodline. You have your mother's posture and proud chin. Now just look up—that's it. Don't look at your feet. You don't want to show that you're intimidated or afraid."

"Should I smile?"

"It doesn't really matter," he said. "Smiling is a human gesture. It won't mean much to most of them, unless they were only turned recently, like Cecile. But new vampires are still susceptible to the spell that protects the city." He glanced at Cecile. "You saw that firsthand."

She nodded. "Do vampires really not smile?"

"We *can*," Cryder said. "But showing teeth tends to mean something a bit different in our culture."

"Your mother—"

"My mother is a diplomat," Cryder said. "That's part of being a ruler. She smiled at you because she knew that was what would make you most comfortable." Then he laughed. "Don't worry. She was never going to eat you."

"I wasn't worried about *that*," I mumbled.

The guests to the palace had taken up positions in a ring around the courtyard. Now they were staring at me and Cryder. "Am I supposed to say something?" I asked.

"No. Just let them see you. Let them understand who you are. And—"

"And what?"

But Cryder seemed unable to say anymore.

"They're scenting you," Drake supplied.

Cryder gave him a dark look.

"*Scenting?*" I felt a shiver come over me. "What does that mean?"

Cryder's arms tightened around me. "Remember how Bristol was able to find you by smelling your blood? And so was I?"

"Yes?"

"They can do the same. They can tell by your scent what you

are and who your mother was." He kissed the crown of my head. "Don't worry. You're perfectly safe. But if they're going to accept you as their new queen, it's something they need to know."

"Will it turn them against me?"

"Not a bit," Cryder assured me. "It will make them trust you more to know that you're one of them."

But I wasn't one of them, was I? Not really. All right, so maybe I had vampire blood. Maybe my mother had been a vampire. But I had been raised in the human world. Even though Cryder had been prepping me for months for my transition to vampire life, I still felt as human as they come.

I knew Cecile had been through a bit of the same thing. We had talked about it the night before graduation, huddled in her bedroom and speculating about all the ways our lives were about to change. "At least you'll be among your own people," I'd said. "You'll be with pure vampires, like you."

She'd laughed. "I'm hardly pure vampire," she'd said. "I mean, I am in all the basic ways, I suppose. I don't sleep anymore. That's pretty bizarre."

And the bloodlust. I hadn't mentioned that aloud, though. Transitioning to a diet of blood had been strange enough for me, and I was just drinking cocktails of Cryder's blood that he'd donated willingly. Cecile, I knew, had far more complicated feelings about her new diet, and I still didn't know whether she was ready to talk about it. She would come to me, I supposed, in her own time.

Until then, I wasn't going to be the one to bring it up. She had been doing a remarkable job adjusting, I thought. After all, this whole situation should never have been her problem in the first place. *She* wasn't the one with a vampire for a mother. *She* wasn't the one being hunted by an evil vampire hell-bent on taking her blood. Her life should have moved seamlessly from high school to college to career, and maybe to becoming a wife and mother.

Well, she'd still have the chance to get married, I thought, noting Drake's hand resting on her shoulder. If nothing else, she'd found love. And I knew from firsthand experience how valuable that could be in a trying time.

Cecile had punched her pillows into a supportive shape and leaned back on them. "I might be a pure-blooded vampire," she'd said, "but I don't belong in their world any more than you do. Probably less. At least your mother was one of them. Me, I'm just a random girl who got in the way of Bristol."

I'd hugged her. "You're not random," I'd told her firmly. "You're my sister, practically. You're my best friend. I need you with me, Cecile."

I was jerked back to the present as Samuele stepped forward and raised both of his hands above his head. All of the vampires standing around us fell silent, waiting to hear what their king would say.

"Citizens of La Oscurità," he began. I was surprised by how well his voice carried. It seemed as though the courtyard we were standing in had somehow been designed for its acoustics. The sound reverberated off the cobblestones.

"Honored guests, beloved friends," Samuele continued. "I welcome you with open arms and open heart to the palace today. We thank you for your attendance. We are humbled by your show of support for your new king and queen."

Cryder's hand slid down to grip mine. It suddenly occurred to me to wonder whether he was nervous.

I'd never seen Cryder nervous. At least, I didn't think I had. But today wasn't just a big deal for me, was it? He was about to succeed his parents as ruler of La Oscurità. He was stepping up to an enormous responsibility, something he'd probably been preparing for all his life. In a way, I was lucky. I was a newcomer to this world, and everyone knew it. No one would expect me to be very good at my new life right out the gate. I would be given time to learn, time to find my footing. But Cryder would have all these eyes watching every move he made.

I squeezed his hand back. For the first time in our entire relationship, I felt like an equal partner. I was afraid, yes, but so was he. I could feel that we were drawing strength from each other.

That was kind of amazing.

He stepped forward, bringing me along with him, and lifted a hand to wave at his congregated people.

I waved too, thinking of photos I'd seen of royal couples together and feeling a little bit foolish. I wasn't a real queen. It felt strange to be acting like one.

Except that, actually, I *was* a real queen, wasn't I? Just a couple of days ago, I'd been graduating from high school. Today I was greeting the town of La Oscurità as their new ruler.

It didn't feel like it could be real life. But it was, and the sooner I got my head around that fact, the happier we'd all be.

"Welcome, Cryder!" Samuele said. "And welcome, Rena!"

There was a moment of silence in which you could have heard a pin drop. My heart seemed to be pounding in my ears.

Then a roar of applause broke over us like a wave. The vampires gathered in the courtyard around us were smiling and cheering, some of them even stamping their feet eagerly on the ground.

Cryder wrapped his arm around me. "They approve," he said quietly into my ear. "We pass the first test."

I laughed with nervous relief.

But this had just been the beginning. I didn't know what lay ahead for me, but I was fairly confident that gaining the approval of the vampires clustered here had been the easy part.

Now the real trials would begin.

Chapter Four

We made our way into the castle, Cryder's parents leading the way, the four of us following after. I did my best not to shrink back into Cryder's arms, to look as though I was comfortable and confident and ready to face whatever was waiting for me inside, but the truth was that I was deeply shaken by what had just happened out in the courtyard

At least I got their approval, I reminded myself. It could have been much worse. What if they'd all just stood there staring stone faced at me and Cryder? What if they'd refused to approve our union, or refused to accept me as queen? What would have happened then? I supposed I would have been put on a plane right back home. Which would mean heading back into danger. Back to a place where rogue vampires like Bristol could find me and hurt me.

I wouldn't have been able to go back to Cecile's mother. Not after what had happened to Cecile herself. I wouldn't be able to stand it if anyone else was hurt because of me, because of what I was. If the vampires hadn't wanted me, I would have had to go on the run by myself. And I knew I wouldn't have been able to fend off any attackers for very long. I wasn't a fighter. I didn't have those skills.

Stop worrying about it, I told myself firmly. I had been approved. I had been accepted. I was here now, and I was to be allowed to stay, and that meant I didn't have to think any more about where I would go if I couldn't be here.

31

It was just that everything was happening so fast.

A gasp from Cecile brought me back to the present. We were standing in a vast open foyer with a marble floor and high columns all the way around the perimeter. It must have been at least three stories high, to judge by the sweeping stone staircase that led up before forking in two divergent directions.

"This is beautiful," Cecile breathed.

She was right. It was absolutely gorgeous. Everything in the foyer seemed to sparkle when the light from outside caught it. Was it all made of marble? It seemed as though it might be.

"Are we really going to live here?" Cecile asked.

"Not right here in the foyer," Samuele laughed warmly. "You'll have living quarters. But yes, you'll be residing in the palace, of course. This is where royalty lives."

"Even me, though?" Cecile asked. "I'm not royalty. I'm just a high school student."

"You graduated," I reminded her. It seemed like something from another life. In a very real way, I guess it was.

"Okay, I graduated," she agreed. "That doesn't make me *royalty*."

"Drake is royalty," Cryder said, smiling at her. "He's a part of my family."

"But again, what does that make me?" Cecile asked. "I'm just dating him. Are you sure I belong here?"

"The palace is the safest place in La Oscurità," Giorgia said. "Don't you want to live here with us?"

"Of course, I do! I just...it all seems too good to be true. A few months ago, I was taking the SATs and applying to state schools, and now this?"

"Why don't we show you around the place," Giorgia suggested. "Perhaps it will begin to feel a bit more like home if you see a little more of it."

"A tour is a wonderful idea," Cryder agreed. His arm rested on my shoulders, securing me to his side. "Shall we begin in the throne room?"

The throne room! I supposed I had known there must be a throne room—this was a palace, after all, and Giorgia and Samuele were the king and queen—but to actually see it would make the whole thing real in a way it hadn't been so far.

Samuele led the way through the foyer to a huge set of double doors. They were bigger than any doors I'd ever seen before—they seemed to stretch for miles above my head. I was sure they'd be too heavy to open, but Samuele managed them with apparent ease.

This time I was the one who gasped.

The throne room was a masterpiece. It was surrounded with stained glass, and the floor was made of tiny golden tiles. At the head of the room stood a raised dais, on which three thrones rested. The two in the center belonged to the king and queen, I was certain, but there was a smaller, slightly less ornate one off to one side. What was that for?

It's Cryder's, I answered my own question. *That's Cryder's throne.*

I pictured the three of them sitting there and felt slightly shivery. This was the royal family of La Oscurità. The royal family of the vampire world. My new world.

And I was one of them now.

Would I be expected to sit in one of those massive thrones, now that Cryder and I were taking over from his parents? The vision in my head shifted, and now I saw myself sitting up there. It was an incongruous thought. This room was far too ornate, too fancy, for someone like me. I didn't belong up on that throne.

"This is where the citizens of La Oscurità come when they have problems that need to be addressed," Giorgia said. "We take meetings with La Oscurità citizens every day. Sometimes there are only a few petitioners. Other days, dozens come. As king and queen, your responsibility will be to hear their grievances and do your best to resolve them."

Cryder nodded, seeming to take that in stride—I supposed he wasn't hearing anything he didn't already know—but I felt shaken. How was I supposed to solve the problems of vampires? I couldn't even imagine what those problems might be, but I felt sure they'd be out of my league.

"Can Rena sit on that throne?" Cecile asked.

"Cecile!" I couldn't believe she was being so forward.

"It'll make a good picture," Cecile said. "We can send it to my mom."

"What are you talking about? We can't send a picture like

that to your mom!"

"Sure, we can," Cecile argued. "We'll just tell her we're touring an old palace. It's the truth. She'll think it's neat, and she won't be worried, and it's something we can actually be kind of honest with her about."

I felt terrible. Cecile had never been anything less than enthusiastic about our new life, but it must be hard for her to be leaving her mother behind. Of course, she would jump at the opportunity to share something. I turned to Giorgia. "Is it okay?"

Giorgia seemed to understand. "It's more than fine," she said gently. "The throne is soon to be yours, after all."

It still didn't feel fine. It felt like trespassing, and I also felt more than a little foolish. But I allowed Cryder to conduct me to the throne, and I allowed Cecile to take a picture of me seated there.

Then, she wanted to do pictures of Cryder and me together, him on his throne and me on mine. Cryder sat down gamely enough and smiled for the photos. I noticed Giorgia and Samuele exchanging looks. Were we embarrassing ourselves? Were we failing to respect the solemnity of the occasion? Or maybe we were just acting too human?

I hopped off the throne and returned to Cecile's side. "Can we see the rest of the palace?" I asked, suddenly eager to put the throne room behind me.

"Of course," Samuele said. "Let's proceed into the ballroom."

The ballroom!

The throne room had overwhelmed me, but it hadn't exactly surprised me—I had known such a thing must exist. It was a palace, after all. Kings and queens had to have audiences with their people *somewhere*. But a ballroom? Such a thing had never even occurred to me. "Are there many balls?" I found myself asking, my curiosity overcoming my shyness.

"A few each year," Giorgia said. "There will be one for your coronation, of course.

I found Cryder's hand. A coronation sounded a bit frightening, but I didn't dare ask for too many details about that just now. "Who comes to them?" I asked instead. "All the people we saw outside, I suppose?"

"Yes," Giorgia said. "All of La Oscurità is welcome at the

royal balls." We had reached another pair of wide double doors, and she threw these open. "The ballroom," she announced.

It was, if that were possible, even more gorgeous than the throne room. It was also much more modern. The floor was made of highly polished wood, and three of the four walls were clear glass, providing stunning views of the grounds. I looked up. The ceiling was peppered with massive skylights. Dancing here would feel like dancing in a snow globe. Nervous as I was about the idea of a coronation, at which I would be the center of attention, I had to admit that I was a little excited about the prospect of a ball.

Adjoining the ballroom was the dining room. This room featured a long oaken table—long enough to seat several dozen diners, I thought. Did vampires really need a dining room? What did they do in here? I had never seen a vampire eat anything I would categorize as food before.

I didn't ask. I admired the room and followed the family back out to the main foyer.

"Upstairs?" Cryder asked me.

I nodded. I did want to see the upper rooms of the palace.

Samuele led the way. "The ground floor is the only one that's ever open to the public," he said. "These rooms up here are all private, for the family's use only." He rested a hand on one of the doors. "I don't know whether you enjoy reading?"

"I do."

"Then you'll want to acquaint yourself with our library. It's one of the finest private collections on the continent. We'll make sure you have some time tomorrow to explore it more fully, if we can." Cecile, I noticed, was wearing a sort of glazed expression, and Samuele smiled indulgently. "I'm sure you girls would like to see your bedroom?"

There would be a bed. I was suddenly aware of just how exhausted I felt. "That would be great," I said.

Samuele led the way to another door. "You and Cecile will share this room, Rena," he said.

I frowned, confused. Though I hadn't really thought about it, I realized now that I had expected to share a room with Cryder. Weren't we to be married, after all? We were going to rule together.

Giorgia seemed to understand my puzzlement. "The royal family is highly scrutinized," she said. "It would be improper for the prince and his bride to be to share quarters before the wedding and coronation. So, until that time, you will stay with your friend."

I nodded assent. I didn't mind, actually. Enough was already changing, what with our having flown to a new country, moved into a palace, and preparing for the rituals that would allow me to take my place as queen. I wasn't sure I was ready to take my relationship with Cryder to the next level on top of all that. For a few nights, at least, it would be a relief to go to sleep with Cecile by my side. It would be something familiar in all of this.

Cryder gave me a quick hug. "Why don't you two get some rest," he suggested. "Tomorrow will be a busy day."

"*Today* was a busy day," I pointed out.

He chuckled. "All the more reason to sleep while you can.

I wanted to kiss him, but I felt funny doing so in front of his parents. Their impression of me was still forming, and I wanted it to be a good one. I settled for returning his hug. Then I thanked the king and queen again and followed Cecile into our new accommodations.

"Oh, look," she said delightedly. "They already brought up our suitcases!"

So they had. The room contained two large, comfortable looking beds, and our bags rested at the foot of each of them. I went to the bed with my own bag and flopped down on my back. "I'm much too tired to unpack tonight," I announced.

"I know what you mean." Cecile dropped into her own bed like a sack of bricks. "I don't even understand how I can be this tired. It's not like I sleep. It's not like my body needs to refresh itself."

"You're emotionally tired," I suggested.

"Okay, Dr. Phil." She rolled up onto one elbow so she could look at me. "What do you suppose they all do at night?" she asked. "I mean, they're not sleeping either, are they?"

"Yeah," I agreed. "It's weird to think about. Like, having eight extra hours in the day. How would you fill all that time?"

"Cryder's never told you what he does?"

"No," I admitted. "But we haven't exactly been hard up for things to talk about in the time we've known each other, you know. I know almost nothing about this world, and now I'm supposed to rule it. That's pretty crazy."

"Yeah," she said. "But hey, Rena, you'll be a queen!"

"You say that like it's a good thing."

"Isn't it?"

"Maybe. How would I know? I never even went to my senior prom, for God's sake."

"Yeah, we probably should have done that."

I had to laugh. "We're not going to be lacking in formal parties to attend," I pointed out to her. "Remember, there's a coronation coming up."

"Do you think I'll be invited?"

"Are you serious?"

"Well, I don't know anything about it either."

"You're Drake's girlfriend. Drake is a member of the royal family, too. Of course, you'll be invited."

"Mmm, you're probably right."

"Besides, they said the entire *town* was invited. All of La Oscurità. They didn't mean all of La Oscurità except you."

She laughed. "I'm being silly, aren't I."

"No sillier than me," I said. "I'm completely in over my head here, Cecile."

"No, you aren't," she protested. "You're going to do fine. You'll be a great queen. I know you're worried that you don't know what you're doing," she cut me off before I could object, "but Cryder *knows* you don't know what you're doing. The whole town of La Oscurità knows. Everyone's going to be patient. And you've got a lot of people here to help you get your feet under you."

"I suppose that's true."

"It is true. And don't forget, you're not going to have to do it alone. You'll have Cryder as your king. And he *does* know what he's doing. He was raised to do this. He's been preparing for it all his life."

Somewhat reassured, I went to my suitcase and changed into my pajamas. Then I got back into bed and pulled the covers up to my chin. The long trip and the journey into the vampire city had definitely gotten the better of me, and all I wanted now was to go to sleep.

Chapter Five

I thought I would never fall asleep—my mind was racing a mile a minute—but eventually I must have drifted off because I awoke to the sound of Cecile talking on her phone.

"You didn't have to stay up, Mom," she said. A long pause. "I know you wanted to talk to us—we wanted to talk to you too, honestly, but it must be one in the morning there."

I waved.

"Rena says hi," Cecile added.

I went to my suitcase and started leafing through my clothes, looking for something to wear that day.

"No, it's all good," Cecile said. "Cryder's parents are really nice. Their home is really quaint." She looked at me and rolled her eyes. She couldn't tell her mother that we were staying in a palace, of course. "Yeah, they're taking good care of us. And we should actually probably get downstairs and be social. I think they have something planned for today."

I felt a fluttering in my stomach. Cecile was only guessing, I knew, but what *did* today hold? Would I be put through the painful and unpleasant trials I'd been vaguely warned about? Would I have to meet more of the public of La Oscurità?

"Okay, Mom," Cecile said. "Love you too. Take care." She

hung up. "You're awake," she said to me.

"Yeah. How was your night?"

"*Long.* You can't imagine. I was going stir crazy in here. And then, I knew the rest of the family was awake somewhere in the house, so we *could* have been hanging out the whole time." She shook her head. "I guess maybe they like having nights to themselves or something. It makes sense that they'd want their downtime."

"You could have woken me up," I offered.

She handwaved that. "You were exhausted. It's good you got some sleep. Do you feel better today?"

"A little. Still anxious, though. I hope nothing too intense is going on today."

"Oh, right!" She jumped up. "Something came for you about an hour ago."

"What?"

She went to one of the two desks in the room and picked up a silver platter with a lid on it. Would this be breakfast? I lifted the lid curiously.

There was no food beneath it. Instead, a small cream-colored envelope sat on a doily. My name was written on the front in script.

"Weird," Cecile commented.

I picked up the envelope, tore it open, and pulled out a card with a note scrawled on it:

Rena,

Please join me for breakfast in the dining room when you wake. Cecile is welcome to come along. This will be a formal affair and is part of the traditional process of joining the royal family.

I look forward to seeing you.

Cordially,

Giorgia

I put the note back on the tray and looked up at Cecile, my hands shaking a little. "A formal breakfast?"

She picked up the note and scanned it. "Looks that way. Good thing we packed some nice dresses, isn't it?"

It had been Cryder who had advised us that our formal dresses would be needed. We had wrapped them in tissue paper and stowed them deep in our suitcases. I hadn't expected to need them so soon, nor had I really anticipated needing more than one. "You're going to want more than just your black cocktail dress when we get there," Cecile had said firmly, pushing armloads of jewel toned dresses on me. "Look, it's better to have and not need, right?"

I hadn't been able to deny that. And now, looking from Giorgia's note to the pile of dresses in my suitcase, I was glad I'd let her have her way. "What am I going to wear?" I asked desperately. "I don't know how formal a formal breakfast is."

"Something classy but not over the top," Cecile advised. She rustled around in my clothes for a moment, then pulled out a knee length dress with an ivory bodice and a pale green skirt. "Here," she said. "This is nice, and it's not an evening gown. Put this on. When you're done, I'll do your hair for you."

Shaky and nervous, I got dressed. When I was done, Cecile—who had dressed in a peach bubble dress—carefully wound my hair up for me and pinned it at the back of my head. "I'm glad you're here," I said. "I don't think I could handle it if I had to do all this by myself."

"You could handle it," Cecile assured me. "It's just nice that you don't have to, that's all. Good to have a friend around. Are you ready to go down?"

"No."

"Okay, well, are you ever going to be ready to go down?"

"No."

"Let's do it, then."

We made our way down the stairs. I'd hoped to run into Cryder and Drake in the hall, to be able to say good morning to them, but there was no sign of them. I slipped my phone out of my pocket and texted him—*going to breakfast now.*

The reply came back only seconds later. *Good luck! I know you'll do well. I love you.*

My throat seemed to swell closed. Cryder was so comforting, and he made me feel so safe. If only he could be here, I knew I would feel so much better. *I miss you*, I texted.

I miss you too. Strange, isn't it? We've only been apart for a few hours.

Feels like longer.

I'll see you tonight and you can tell me all about your day.

That promise was enough to make me feel a little better. I just had to get through the next few hours, and then I would be able to spend time with him again.

We finally reached the dining room. The low, gloomy lighting of the day before, had been supplanted with bright overhead lights, and the whole thing was much less spooky because of it. Giorgia sat at the table, a newspaper spread open in front of her. She looked up as we came in, then got to her feet.

"Welcome, ladies," she said. "Please, take a seat. I'm so glad to have you join me for this meal, Rena."

Personally, I was feeling extremely awkward. I was the only one at the table who actually ate food. I was used to meals with Cecile—they were mostly humorous affairs, with her lamenting the fact that she could no longer enjoy her favorite dishes as she once had. But what would eating in front of Giorgia be like?

My question was quickly answered. No sooner had I take a seat at the table than a butler set a plate down in front of me. Eggs, pancakes, bacon, potatoes—it was as good as the best breakfast I'd ever had at home. I dug in quickly, realizing suddenly how very hungry I was. I hadn't eaten anything since the plane.

"Would you like some coffee?" Giorgia asked.

"Please."

"Henry?"

The butler left the room and returned moments later with a carafe. He poured me a piping hot cup. I lifted it to my lips and sipped. It was wonderful.

"Now then," Giorgia said, settling back into her seat. Her dress was pleated and lemon yellow, and it seemed to settle around her like flower petals. "We have a very busy day ahead," she went on. "The men are off touring the city today—that's also tradition, and it will be part of our day too."

"Why didn't we just go together?" Cecile asked. Immediately, she looked mortified. "I'm sorry. I don't mean to be rude—"

"Not at all," Giorgia assured her. "This is your home, Cecile, and I want you to feel free to speak up and ask questions here. You mustn't be intimidated just because of our station."

Cecile nodded hesitantly. I was fairly sure it was going to take a lot more than a basic *don't be intimidated* to bring either one of us fully out of our shells here, but it was a nice sentiment.

"The answer to your question," Giorgia said, "is that this tradition dates back centuries, back to a time when it was considered inappropriate for courting men and women to spend any time together unchaperoned. It became commonplace for the king to take young gentlemen out to introduce them to their responsibilities as ascending ruler, while the queen would introduce young ladies. This was true whether it was a man or a woman marrying into the family. Of course, we all know that you and Cryder have been spending plenty of time together in the States," she laughed. "But we do like to keep our traditions here in La Oscurità."

"That makes sense," I agreed, even though I wished I could have spent the day with Cryder. This was my first full day in Rome, after all, and my first day as part of the vampire world. Having him at my side would have been more than just comforting; it would have been a lot of fun.

But at least I was allowed to be with Cecile. "What will we be doing today?" I asked Giorgia, taking another sip of my coffee.

"After you're done eating, Rena," Giorgia said, "we'll begin the day with a tour of La Oscurità. You'll have a chance to see all the most important and ancient buildings in the city, of course, but we'll be looking at some of the more modern structures too."

"There are modern buildings in La Oscurità?" Cecile asked.

Giorgia laughed kindly. "But of course. Surely, you've noticed that there are modern elements to the palace itself? This city has only grown over the past century."

"How could it have grown?" I asked. "If new people can't ever move here—"

"But they can," Giorgia said, looking just as surprised as I felt. "New people move to La Oscurità all the time. The two of you, for example."

"But we're a special case, aren't we?" I was confused. "Cryder said there were wards around the city—"

"The protective enchantments only keep humans out," Giorgia said.

Feeling slightly embarrassed, I put it together. "New vampires."

"La Oscurità is one of the safest and most welcoming places on earth for vampires," Giorgia said. "There are other communities here and there, in other countries. But when someone is new to the vampire world, we always hope they'll find their way here. It's a good place to adjust to the new life."

The idea of an influx of newly created vampires made me anxious. Older vampires, like the royal family, had adjusted to this life and were settled into their ways. But weren't the newer ones more likely to be wild? More likely to be like Bristol had been?

I checked myself. Cecile was a new vampire and *she* wasn't a murderous animal. I was allowing my fear to rule me. I forced myself to try to accept the idea of new vampires as something good, an addition to our community as opposed to a threat.

"Will we get to meet any of them?" Cecile asked. She clearly wasn't having the same apprehensive reaction to the idea of new vampires that I'd had. If anything, she looked excited. I couldn't really blame her, either—these were her people, after all. Of course, she would want to meet them and learn more about them.

Giorgia nodded. "As we move around the city, we'll be greeting the citizens," she said. "We always try to make sure we get plenty of face time with the people. The last thing we want is to become distant rulers, lording over them from afar and never connecting with their needs or problems. And of course, everyone will want to meet Rena." She smiled at me.

My nerves escalated. "They're going to want to meet me?"

"But of course. You're about to become their new queen, after all."

"Am I supposed to say something to them?" Last night's audience with the people of La Oscurità had been stressful enough, and I'd only had to stand there and look decent for that one.

"You don't have to have a speech prepared," Giorgia assured me. "They might want to converse with you a little. They'll want to know your background, what you're like, what brings you here. Things of that nature. And they'll like to see that you're interested in them and their lives. Everyone wants to feel important. If they see that their new queen is someone who wants to listen to them, they'll be happy."

That didn't sound so bad. It seemed like I might be able to do more listening than talking. And I had to admit, I *was* curious about La Oscurità and its people. It would be interesting to hear what they had to say about the city and about their lives here.

And, of course, there was Cecile to think of. She was practically bouncing up and down in her chair at the thought of meeting more vampires and learning about how they lived.

It occurred to me that we knew very little about authentic vampire life. We'd been close with Cryder and Drake for a while now, but they had been living in *our* world. Now the tables had turned. What would we discover when we went out into the city and met the vampires up close?

Giorgia was still laying out the day for us. "While we're out, we'll stop for lunch," she said.

"Lunch?" I blinked. "There aren't any humans in this city. What are we going to have for lunch?"

She hesitated. "I believe you've been drinking blood? Given by Cryder?"

"Yeah, but not, like, *exclusively*. Are you saying we're having a liquid lunch?"

She gave another of her high, tinkling laughs. "A liquid lunch! I like that. You're a laugh, Rena! Yes, I suppose that's what I'm saying. Now that you're here and you're transitioning into life with us, it's important for you to begin your dietary transition too."

That didn't sound so great. I'd had Cryder's blood cocktails, yes, but only when I was at home alone with no one to judge my reaction to them. The idea of drinking blood while out on the town—and having all my new subjects watching me while I did it— was fairly horrifying.

"We'll be back here in time for dinner," Giorgia assured me. "And dinner will include human food. We know your body still needs that."

Well, that was something.

"And before we sit down to dinner," Giorgia went on, "we'll have a discussion of the trials."

"The trials." I felt as if I'd missed a step going down.

"Cryder told you about them, I'm sure?"

"He didn't give me any details." My heart was pounding. The only thing I knew for sure was that it was going to be painful, whatever it was. I didn't feel at all ready to face that.

But it looked as if there was no putting it off. We were going to talk about it tonight. In a way, it was a relief—finally I would know what I was facing.

But in another way, it wasn't a relief at all. I would have to acknowledge what lay ahead, no matter how horrifying it might be. I would have to go in with my eyes wide open.

I was completely out of my depth here.

Chapter Six

Cecile and I were sent to change our clothes before our tour of La Oscurità. The wardrobe change surprised me—it had been so important for us to dress formally; I had assumed we would need our dresses for more than just breakfast with Cryder's mother. But Cecile seemed to take it in stride.

"Of course, we're not going to tour the town in our formalwear," she laughed, pulling on a pair of comfortable jeans. "We need clothes we can walk in, even if you *are* the queen to be."

"So, you think it's fine if I just wear pants and a sweater?"

"Totally. Go for it."

"I don't know what I'd do without you," I admitted, pulling my most comfortable hoodie over my head.

"Luckily, you're never going to have to find out," Cecile said. "Everything that's happened in the last few months has been pretty weird, but one of my favorite parts of it all is the fact that our lives are stuck together forever."

"They always were!" I protested. "You're like a sister to me, Cecile. Nothing was ever going to come between the two of us."

"Okay, that's true," Cecile said. "But you know what I mean. Sisters grow apart sometimes, or they move to different parts of the world. But you and I are always going to be together, because of this whole vampire thing."

I loved how casual she could be about it. *This whole vampire thing*. To me it was a huge, monumental, overwhelming turn of events that constantly threatened to send me reeling. But Cecile seemed to view it as just the next phase in her life. Some girls go to college after high school, other girls are bitten by vampires and fly off to Rome to join the royal family of the undead.

We met up with Giorgia in the foyer. She was dressed down too, although not as much as we were. I didn't know if I could have processed the sight of Giorgia in jeans and a hoodie. She smiled when she saw us and extended an arm toward the door. "Our carriage awaits."

Are we really taking a carriage? I followed her outside expecting to see a horse drawn vehicle in the driveway. Instead, our conveyance turned out to be a limousine. Cecile squealed happily and clapped her hands, then ran over and climbed into the back.

I followed her in, and Giorgia joined us. There was a small refrigerator in the back of the limo, and as we pulled away Giorgia reached in and pulled out three opaque bottles. "Drinks," she said. "We'll need our energy today."

"What are they?" I asked, accepting the one she handed to me.

"You can't smell it?" Cecile asked.

I twisted the cap off my drink and inhaled. It was bitter and rusty, yet somehow appealing at the same time. "I don't know what this is."

"It's blood," Cecile said gently. "You need to get used to incorporating this into your diet, Rena. I know Cryder started giving you blood before you left the United States, isn't that right?"

"Yes," I admitted. "But I thought that was just to cure the illness I was suffering from at the time."

"You're transitioning," she said. "You're taking on more and more of the characteristics of a vampire. Part of that means drinking blood. Your body needs this for sustenance."

Cecile took a long swig from her own bottle. "Have I got a blood mustache?" she asked me.

She did. "You're something else," I told her, and took a slow and careful sip from my own bottle.

To my surprise, the drink actually tasted good. Intellectually, I knew there was something wrong about it—it wasn't as if it tasted sweet. But I liked it, nonetheless. It was like my body knew that this was something I needed and was encouraging me to drink it.

I must be farther along in my transition to full vampire than I thought, I realized. *I found the blood gross and creepy when Cryder gave it to me. Now, I actually sort of like it.* That idea freaked me out, but I knew I needed to try to be more like Cecile. I needed to embrace what was happening to me, the new life I'd been invited into.

We spent the day touring La Oscurità, stopping frequently to get out of the car and say hello to a passersby. I was constantly amazed by how excited everyone seemed to be to meet me. I was awkward the first couple of times someone came up to introduce themselves, but then I got into the swing of it and even began to enjoy the process. I met people who had been living in La Oscurità for centuries, and a few newcomers as well. Some of the newer vampires acted as happy and intrigued by their new lives as Cecile did, but others seemed more like me—wary and uncertain.

Giorgia showed us all the beautiful architecture of La Oscurità as well. "All of these buildings have been here since Rome itself was built," she said, gesturing around the beautiful piazza at the center of town. "We update them from time to time, make sure they remain functional, but the appearance of this piazza hasn't changed in all that time."

"Wow." I was impressed. "Humans don't do that. So much of Rome itself has aged and fallen to ruin."

"Humans don't understand the passage of time the way we do," Giorgia said. "The human lifespan is so short, much shorter than the lifespan of most buildings. Often, it simply doesn't occur to them to preserve or update a structure until it's too late. Of course, I believe you face this issue less often in America," she said, issuing one of her high, tinkling laughs. "All your buildings are so new!"

It's not something I've ever thought about before, but she's right. Everything in America is relatively new, relatively young. And now I've left that life behind and come to a land that's tied directly to ancient history.

Pretty fitting, considering.

As the day drew to a close, we returned to the palace and went back to our suite for the third wardrobe change of the day, this time into casual cocktail dresses. We joined Giorgia in the parlor. I half hoped to see Cryder and Drake waiting there for us too—I was surprised by how much I missed Cryder, even after only a few hours apart—but there was no sign of them. *Damn.*

Giorgia indicated two seats by the fire, and Cecile and I took them. "I've sent down to the kitchen for some hot tea," she told me. "I thought you might like something a little more familiar to you than blood while we discuss what's next for you," she said.

"Oh. Yeah. I mean, yes, thank you," I stammered. *The trials.* She was talking about the trials. I had been dreading this. As much as I hated not knowing what was coming, there was comfort in it too. While the trials remained unspecified, it was easy to pretend they weren't really going to happen.

"You're nervous," Giorgia observed.

"Yes, ma'am." Of course, I was nervous. Cryder had said the trials would be painful. I didn't want to suffer.

Giorgia nodded. "I wish I could tell you that there was nothing to worry about, but the truth is that the trials are difficult. Not just anybody can make it through. The purpose of these exercises is to elevate future rulers above the rest of the vampire population, and as such, you must have something special in order to get through."

"So, you went through these trials?" Cecile asked.

"I did," Giorgia said. "So did every ruler ever to preside over La Oscurità."

"How many trials are there?" I asked, dreading the answer.

"There are three," Giorgia said, and for a moment I felt a sense of relief. *Only three?* I had imagined a long process stretching out for weeks, maybe even months. I had imagined my entire life being taken over by this torturous testing. It seemed as though, one way or another, it might at least be over quickly.

"The trials are designed to test you in three fundamental

ways," Giorgia said, nodding thanks to a servant as the tea tray was brought in. She poured a cup and passed it over to me, but I couldn't bring myself to drink. I just held the tea cradled in my hands, drawing comfort from its warmth. "The first trial will assess your mental abilities. You will be faced with questions and requests from the people of La Oscurità and asked to resolve them. Judgment will be made based on how well you do."

"Hang on," I objected. "You're going to have me make decisions that will actually impact these people's lives *before* I've passed the trials?" I wasn't sure I was ready for something like that. "What if I choose wrong?"

"Nothing to worry about," Giorgia assured me. "The trials are just tests, Rena. Just simulations. You'll be making your choices in a virtual reality chamber, and we'll be evaluating your responses, but there will be no impact on the real citizens of La Oscurità."

"Well, that doesn't sound so bad," Cecile said. "She just has to pass the test."

It sounded plenty stressful to me. If I made the wrong choices, I would fail, and then what? But Cecile was right that it didn't sound as bad as anything I had been imagining. It wasn't going to be painful. It would just be anxiety-inducing, like every other test I'd ever had in my life.

Still...Giorgia had mentioned three trials. "What's the second trial?" I asked.

"The second trial tests you physically," Giorgia said.

I frowned. "I'm not an athlete. I never have been."

"That isn't a problem," Giorgia said. "When your full vampire abilities come in, you'll be much stronger, faster, and more agile than you are now."

Which was great, but I didn't have those abilities yet. How was I going to pass this trial while I was still part human?

Cecile seemed to be thinking along the same lines. "That's not fair," she said. "You can't ask Rena to pass a trial designed to test vampire skills before she's finished her transition. There's no way she'll be able to do it." She glanced at me. "Sorry, Rena."

"Don't apologize." I was glad she'd spoken up. She'd saved

me from having to say it.

"Not to worry," Giorgia said smoothly. "We'll inject you with a serum that will temporarily grant you full vampire abilities. You'll be physically capable of completing the trial, but we'll be evaluating your reaction time and your ability to trust yourself. It will be difficult, since you're not accustomed to having this extra strength, but a royal must be able to rely on him- or herself."

That sounded a little more intimidating than the first trial. In the first one, I would just be using logic to make decisions. I'd been doing that all my life. But the second trial would require me to utilize skills I'd never had before. "What's the third trial?" I asked, already fearing the answer.

"The third trial tests your emotional ability," Giorgia said. She spoke softly now, and I could tell that for the first time since I'd arrived, she was truly being gentle with me. "You'll come face to face with the greatest trauma of your past, and your response will be evaluated. A ruler must have the ability to overcome great emotional strife."

The greatest trauma of my past.

I knew instantly what that would be. The death of my parents.

It was something I didn't like to think about, because every time I did, I felt as though I was going to fall apart. But in the third trial, I wouldn't be able to fall apart. I would have to face the horror of my parents' death and be strong.

I don't know if I can do this.

Chapter Seven

Thank God for Cecile. She seemed to understand immediately how freaked out I was by everything Giorgia was saying. She had always been able to read me like a book, and I truly didn't know how I would have been able to manage my new life without her.

It's hard to say you're grateful that your best friend has been turned into a vampire. The thought made me feel selfish and uncaring. But I couldn't deny that I was overwhelmingly glad to have her with me, and I knew I always would be.

As Giorgia finished describing the trials, Cecile slid closer to me on the couch, her shoulder pressing into mine, giving me comfort. She might as well have been talking to me, whispering words of encouragement, telling me that she knew I could get through the trials. I felt immediately bolstered. She had always been able to do this when I'd felt anxious or upset. She really was as close and as wonderful as a sister to me.

The only thing that would have been better would have been having Cryder there too. I was shocked by how much I had come to depend on him in the short time we'd known each other. But he was every bit as skilled as Cecile was at calming me down and making me feel safe. I wished he were with us now.

Why on Earth had this day's activities been split up along gender lines? Another vampire tradition, I supposed. Thanks to my upbringing—the loss of my parents at a young age and my incorporation into my best friend's family—I'd never had a lot of traditions that I clung to. I knew other people found them important and reassuring, but I didn't really get what the fuss was about. I would have felt better if my boyfriend—my fiancé—was here. It sucked that he had to be apart from me because of some tradition.

Don't dwell, I told myself firmly. *Make the most of this time with the queen.* It was an opportunity to learn more about what my future held, after all, and that was important. I should take advantage of it, not just moon around about Cryder.

Cecile seemed to be thinking along the same lines. "Why does La Oscurità need a new king and queen anyway?" she asked. "I've never really understood that. I mean, in the human world there has to be a line of succession in case the royals die, but you and Samuele aren't dying."

Giorgia favored us with a chuckle. "No, we're not," she agreed. "But ruling is hard work, and eventually every ruler wants to step aside. Samuele and I have decided that time has come for us. We're well over a hundred years old, you know."

I'd actually had no idea how old she was. It hadn't seemed polite to ask. She looked as if she could be any age—twenty-three or forty-four or seventy. It was something about the clear skin and youthful features combined with the wise expression and the dignified way she carried herself. "I guess if I'd been doing something for that long, I might want some downtime too," I said.

"And eventually you will," Giorgia agreed. "Eventually you will have had enough of ruling, and you'll be ready to pass the crown to whomever comes next. Samuele and I are looking forward to a long vacation together. A quiet retirement."

Cecile burst out laughing. Even I had to smile. "I'm sorry," Cecile giggled. "It's just that hearing you talk about retirement like that—you sound so normal."

"So human, you mean?"

"Yes," Cecile said. "But I mean *normal* too. I don't just

mean you sound mortal, and like you're not a vampire. I mean you sound like you're not a queen. It's hard to imagine a queen talking about retirement."

"I guess most of them probably don't," I pointed out. "Human queens rule for life."

"Exactly," Cecile said.

"You can see why that sort of arrangement makes less sense for us, though," Giorgia said. "It isn't just because our rulers tire of ruling after a while. The people of La Oscurità appreciate having new rulers. New ideas. It's the only way anything ever changes around here."

"I think I understand," I said.

"Very good," Giorgia said, smiling. "I've had a wonderful time with you girls today. I want to thank you for spending your day with me. It's been so long since I've met anyone who's new to this life, and it's very refreshing to speak to young people." She smiled at me and took my hand. "I think Cryder made a wonderful choice in you, dear. The people of La Oscurità are going to get a splendid new queen. I know you'll do a good job tomorrow."

"Tomorrow?" A chill ran down my spine. She couldn't possibly mean what I thought she meant, could she?

"The trials will begin first thing tomorrow morning," Giorgia said. She sounded almost apologetic, as if she knew exactly how hard those words would be for me to hear.

"That's probably good, right?" Cecile asked, leaning her shoulder into mine a little harder. "The sooner they start, the sooner they'll be over, and you won't have to worry about them."

I knew she was right. It would be good to have the trials behind me, and to move on to whatever came next. But at the same time, it was hard to face the fact that the terrifying things Giorgia had told me about would be starting *tomorrow*. I wouldn't have any time to study or to prepare myself. I was just going to be thrown in, and I would either have to handle it or not.

I supposed that was the point. If I couldn't do it without a bunch of preparation, I probably couldn't do it at all.

"You'd better get some sleep," Giorgia said. "You've got an

early day tomorrow.

It was all I could do to nod and allow Cecile to lead me from the room.

***

"Rena?" Cecile said quietly. "Are you up for a visitor?"

I had been lying on my bed, staring at the ceiling and willing sleep to come for me, for the past half hour. Now I glanced over at my friend. She was watching me apprehensively, as if she was afraid I might completely freak out at any minute.

"It's Cryder," she said.

If anyone in the world could make me feel better about what I was facing, I knew it was him. "Yes," I said. "Yeah. I want to see Cryder." I sat up and did my best to arrange my hair in something resembling a style.

Cryder came in. He was dressed more casually than I'd ever seen him in my life, in flannel pants and a white t-shirt, and he sat down on the bed beside me and pulled me into his arms. I was immediately comforted. He was a reminder of the fact that not everything about this new world was strange and frightening. Some aspects of it had been wonderful.

"I missed you today," he said quietly, smoothing my hair, his skilled fingers having much more success at taming it than mine had.

"What did you do?" I asked, longing for a distraction.

"Not much," he said. "Went around La Oscurità and saw the people. It wasn't a formal tour, like you and Cecile got. Drake and I grew up here, so we know the city just fine. But we saw some of the old familiar sights, and that was nice. Did you have a good time with my mother?"

"She was very kind," I said.

"You're nervous." He stroked my hair gently.

"Is it that obvious?"

"Your heart's beating really fast." He slid two fingers down the line of my jaw and brought them to rest on my neck, feeling my pulse. "You need to try to relax, Rena, or you'll never get any sleep."

"There's no way I'm going to be able to relax," I said. "The trials are tomorrow. Did you know they were going to be tomorrow?"

He hesitated. "I did," he said finally.

I sat up. "You knew? And you didn't tell me? You didn't prepare me at all?"

"Rena, there was nothing I could have done about it," he said. "There was nothing I could have done to help you feel better prepared. You always would have been feeling like this. And I didn't want you to spend more time than necessary worrying about it. I wanted you to be able to have fun on your first day in La Oscurità. You don't really wish you'd spent the whole day thinking about the trials, do you?"

"I suppose not," I admitted begrudgingly.

"Besides," he said, "you're going to be fine. I have faith in you."

"Did your mother have to face trials?"

"Of course. Every potential ruler does."

"Did you?"

"Yes, but I faced them before you knew me," he said. "When I was younger. Years ago."

"You were a child?"

He laughed. A moment later I realized my mistake. "No. Of course you weren't."

"I was the age I am now," he said. "Physically speaking, at least. Mentally speaking. I was old enough to take on the challenges of the trials."

"And you passed."

"And so did my mother," he said. "And so did my father."

"Has Drake done it?"

"No," Cryder said. "Drake never considered challenging for the throne. If he had wanted to stake a claim, he would have had to face the trials." He hesitated. "My aunt tried it. My mother's sister."

I knew without asking how that story was going to end, and I was sure I didn't want to hear it, but I couldn't hold back from asking. "She didn't pass, did she? That's why she didn't assume the throne in your mother's place?"

"That's right," Cryder said.

"Tell me about her."

He shook his head. "It isn't important, Rena. You don't want to hear this story right now You should be getting some rest instead."

"Cryder, there's no way I'm going to be able to sleep tonight and you know it. I'm much too nervous. If you tell me about your aunt, at least I'll be able to relax a little bit."

"Okay," he said. His voice held a note of reluctance. "But you have to understand, Rena, what happened with her—it wasn't the norm. She was never supposed to undergo the trials. My mother had been chosen for the throne, and my aunt sought it because she was selfish and power hungry. She didn't care about the people of La Oscurità."

"What happened?"

"Well, she couldn't complete the third trial," Cryder said. "The emotional trial."

"The one where she would have come face to face with the trauma of her past?" I asked, remembering Giorgia's harrowing description.

"That's right. I don't know what she saw—the trials are conducted privately—but whatever it was, she was unable to overcome it."

"So, what happened to her?" A terrible thought suddenly occurred to me. "It didn't kill her, did it?"

"No, no, it didn't kill her." Cryder bit his lip. "It drove her mad."

I felt a wash of horror pass through me. "What do you mean?"

"She was never the same again," Cryder said quietly. "Before the trials, she was vain and self-centered, but she was also exceedingly clever. Afterward, she was a shell of her former self. It was as if the woman she had been, was lost."

"Is she still here?" I asked. "Does she still live in La Oscurità?"

"She does," Cryder said. "But she doesn't visit the palace anymore. She's been committed to a psychiatric ward."

I felt as if I was floating upward, away from my bed, away from my body. "Cryder," I whispered.

His hand came to rest atop mine. "That won't happen to you," he said. "You're stronger than she ever was."

"What if I'm not?"

He kissed me gently, but I couldn't lose myself in the pleasure of his lips. If I had had any other choice, I knew, I would have backed out right then. I would have refused to participate in the trials and gone back home to the States.

But dangerous vampires awaited me there. This was the only place that was safe. This life was my only choice.

Provided I could survive.

Chapter Eight

Dear Rena—
Please dress comfortably today and join us in the dining room for breakfast. We look forward to your arrival. Do not worry—everyone has great confidence in your ability to do well today!
Giorgia

I crumpled the note in my hand as I watched Cecile whirl around the room, getting ready. Her note hadn't said to dress comfortably. She had been told to wear something semi-formal. Even though I was happiest in my sweats, I wished today that I could have traded places with her. I would much rather be putting my hair up and picking out a dress than facing down the ordeal of the trials.

"Are you ready to go?" she asked me, finishing up the application of her mascara.

I nodded. I wasn't ready—I didn't think I would ever be ready—but what could I say? If I didn't go down to breakfast, they would probably come up and get me. There was no avoiding this. And I didn't want to embarrass Cryder. I wanted him to think he'd made the right choice in bringing me home. *I can handle this*, I told myself over and over. *It's just a few tests, and I've always been good at tests. I can take whatever they can dish out.*

God, I hoped that was true.

The whole family was waiting down in the dining room. Giorgia and Samuele smiled as I entered, presumably to help put me at my ease, and Cryder got to his feet and embraced me. "We've got everything you could possibly want for breakfast," he said, guiding me to the table. "I want you to have some blood and some human food, okay? Make sure you're as strong as possible on both fronts."

I nodded, unable to speak, and allowed him to fill my plate with eggs and bacon and to pass me a cup that I knew by smell contained blood. I ate mechanically, cutting my food into manageable bites and transferring it slowly into my mouth. Everything tasted like sand. I was sure on some level that it was very good, but I couldn't bring myself to care.

"We'll go in for the trials first thing after breakfast," Giorgia said. She was speaking softly, kindly, and I knew she could tell I was nervous. "The room is already prepared for you."

"Will we be able to stay with her?" Cecile asked. I was grateful. That was what I'd wanted to know too, but forming words felt impossible right now.

"Regrettably not," Giorgia said. "But you'll all be able to stay in an adjoining room, and you'll know what's going on and how well Rena is doing. If anything should go wrong—not that it will—you'll be able to be at her side in a matter of seconds."

Nothing will go wrong, I told myself. But I couldn't turn my thoughts away from the story Cryder had told me last night about his aunt who had insisted on undergoing the trials and had failed miserably. She was insane now. What if that happened to me?

Cryder continued to urge me to eat, but I felt as if I couldn't keep anything down. The last thing I wanted was to throw up when I was supposed to be completing the trials. Finally, seeing that food had stopped disappearing from my plate, Samuele got to his feet.

"It's time," he said quietly.

Around me, everyone else rose. Cecile rested a hand briefly on my shoulder as she got up. Cryder wrapped his arm around my waist, and I was glad of it. I felt as though I might actually pass out from fear if he wasn't holding me up.

We made our way down a long and narrow hallway that seemed to twist and turn into the very heart of the palace. This hadn't been on our tour. It was intimidating. I wasn't sure that I would have been able to find my way out if I'd been called upon to do so. *Of course, who knows what state I'll be in when the time comes to leave here?*

At least, one way or another, it would all be over.

The room we entered didn't look as if it ought to belong to the palace at all. The elegant decor that was present throughout the rest of the building was absent here. This room would have been more at home in a doctor's office. The walls were sleek and plain white, and the room was completely unfurnished except for a bed in the center. Around the bed was an array of medical equipment that I didn't recognize or understand. It terrified me.

"It's time to say goodbye," Giorgia said. "I'll be here with you, Rena, administering the trials. But everybody else will have to retire to the next room."

Cecile stepped forward and hugged me. "I know you can do this," she said. "You're one of the toughest people I've ever met in my life, Rena. You can get through anything. Just be strong."

I nodded, returning her embrace. It was so reassuring to have someone here who believed in me, even though I thought she was vastly overestimating me. I hoped she was right, though. I hoped I would be able to get through this, and that I wouldn't disgrace myself.

She stepped back, and Cryder came forward. He wrapped me tightly in his arms. I inhaled the scent of him, wishing I could just stay here in his embrace forever. This was the safest place left in my world.

"You know I wouldn't let you do it if I thought anything bad was going to happen to you," Cryder said.

I nodded, even though the truth was more complicated. He had brought me here to get me away from the dangers that faced me at home. This was less dangerous than that. At least here nobody was *trying* to kill me.

But that didn't mean everything was going to be okay.

"All right," Samuele said. "Cryder, Drake, Cecile—come with me."

They looked over their shoulders, waving as they went. A moment later, I was alone. Only Giorgia remained beside me.

"Lie down," she said gently. "Get comfortable on the bed."

"Will the trials take place in bed?"

Giorgia nodded. "Remember how I described them to you as a simulation? You'll be injected with a serum that will cause you to experience certain scenarios. Your test will be in how you respond to those scenarios."

I frown. "I'm going to hallucinate?" I wasn't such a fan of that idea, especially given the fact that my life had taken a sharp turn for the surreal over the last several months. I had become a pretty big fan of clinging to the knowledge that, as weird as things around me might seem, I knew what was real and what wasn't.

"It won't be a genuine hallucination," Giorgia said. "Think of it as more like a projection. We'll be playing images for you in your mind. You'll know what's real and what isn't, and nothing will actually be able to hurt you. It's really the safest and least invasive way we can do this, I promise. You don't have anything to be afraid of.

I still didn't feel great about what lay ahead, but what could I do? The trials were necessary if I wanted to move forward to a life with Cryder. And I did.

I crossed the room and climbed up onto the bed, feeling deeply weird. It was as vulnerable as lying down for an exam at the doctor's office, except that at the doctor's office you weren't literally in bed, and that somehow made the whole thing feel even more vulnerable.

At least Giorgia had a good bedside manner. She moved efficiently, readying equipment I didn't recognize, breaking from her work occasionally to give me a little smile. I believed she really wanted me to do well, and that was immeasurably helpful.

"Okay," she said, placing a mask over my nose and mouth. "You'll be out in a minute. You're just going to feel a quick jab—

that's the serum—and then the first simulation will begin. I'll be right here the whole time, and your friends are waiting in the other room. Not to worry."

My last thought was of Cryder's aunt, the one who had failed her trials and was now insane. It seemed to me that there was plenty to worry about. But before I could articulate the thought, before I could even fully think it, I felt a sharp pain in my arm. The world tilted sideways, and I slid off.

***

I stood in a gown of pale gold at the center of a vast chamber, a crown atop my head. It took me a moment to recognize the room. *The throne room.* Of course.

It's a simulation, I reminded myself. *In this simulation, I'm already queen.* I moved slowly across the room and toward the throne, taking a seat, looking out over the empty space.

"Supplicant number six hundred and forty-five," a disembodied voice said.

The doors swung open. A man entered. As he approached the throne, I understood that he must be a vampire. He stopped before me and bowed. "Your highness."

"Um. Hello." I wasn't sure of the proper greeting. Would that cause me to fail the trial? It couldn't, surely?

"Your highness, I seek your permission to bring a new citizen into our town," the man said.

Why was that a problem? There must be something I didn't know. "Who is this citizen?"

"She is a human woman," he said. "I have fallen in love with her, and she with me."

"I see." That ought to be okay, surely? That was what had happened with Cecile and Drake. But then I remembered something. Cecile hadn't been turned into a vampire until she'd been at death's door from her injuries. She'd had no other choice. And I had been told that only vampires could live in this city. "This woman you speak of—is it your intention to turn her?"

"Yes, Your Majesty."

"And is that her wish as well?"

The man hesitated.

"Is there a problem?"

"It's just that...she doesn't know. What I am."

Oh boy. "And yet you say she's in love with you? How can she love you if she doesn't know the most basic information about who you are?"

"Please, Your Majesty. If I turn her, she'll see all of this from the right perspective."

"Because you will have removed her choices." I shook my head. "No. I forbid this. You must tell this woman the truth if you wish to turn her. Offer her a choice. If she chooses this life freely, then she is welcome here."

The man looked crestfallen, but he appeared to accept my judgment. He left the throne room, shoulders slumped.

The doors swung open again. This time Cryder entered. I wanted to run to him, but something held me back. *It's an illusion*, I reminded myself. He wasn't Cryder. Not quite. Not exactly.

"My queen," he said formally. "May I escort you to the ball?"

I got to my feet. I would have followed Cryder anywhere. Even this shade of Cryder, who wasn't the real thing, was comforting and familiar. I took his arm and allowed him to draw me out of the throne room and into the ballroom.

The ballroom was full of people dancing, gliding in neat circles. Cryder took me in his arms and guided us into a slow waltz. I stepped carefully. I wasn't a good dancer, but by keeping my attention on what I was doing, I managed not to embarrass myself.

"Here's Lady Fiona and her husband, Lord Harrison," Cryder murmured as we came up alongside a man and woman in red wine-colored formalwear.

I knew instinctively what I needed to do. "Good evening My Lord, My Lady," I said politely. "Welcome to the palace. It's so good of you to join us."

"Congratulations on your coronation, Your Highness," Lady

Fiona said. Lord Harrison bowed his head.

Cryder whirled me away—

And then I was rising, ascending through smoke and mist and into darkness.

***

My eyelids felt as if they weighed a ton. I couldn't move.

"No one's ever completed the first task so quickly," a voice said. "She has a preternatural gift for diplomacy. She'll make a good queen. There's no doubt about that."

"If she survives," said a second voice.

"Don't talk like that. She will."

And then another voice, a different voice, much closer. "Rena? Can you hear me?"

"Mmm."

"The first trial is complete. You did well. The second one is about to begin."

I felt another jab in my arm and slipped away again.

Chapter Nine

I waited for the next trial to come into being around me, but it didn't happen. Nothing appeared before me. I didn't find myself in the throne room or anywhere else. Instead, I remained surrounded by blackness.

And pain shot through me like a poison.

I wanted to scream, but I couldn't move. I felt tethered to my bed. Something had gone wrong. I was burning up. My skin was on fire, my very *blood* was ablaze. I wanted to scream, but I couldn't manage it.

This is how I die, I realized. *This is it. Something's gone wrong with the test, and I can't tell them. I'm going to burn alive right here on this table, and nobody's going to know until it's too late.*

Then, as suddenly as it had begun, the burning pain washed away.

It was as if a cool wave of lake water had swept through my body, extinguishing the pain and the poison, bringing me back to the self I knew. I lay still for a long moment, collecting myself, trying to gather my wits, trying to understand what had just happened to me.

The second trial was supposed to be a physical challenge. I knew that, but I had expected some sort of fitness test. But maybe I'd been thinking about it wrong. Maybe the test was to see how well I would hold up under torture.

If so, had I failed? I hadn't been asked any questions, but I felt as though I would have rolled over on my best friend to make that pain go away.

I opened my eyes, fully expecting to see Giorgia, hoping for an explanation of what had just happened to me.

But I didn't see Giorgia. I didn't even see the room I had been ushered into for the trials. Instead, I was standing on the street of an unfamiliar city, watching as cars rushed by at top speed and people—human people—walked past me in a great hurry.

How did I know they were human? Was it just that we were so clearly in a human city?

No. There was something else.

I could *see* them in a way I'd never been able to see people before. There was a quality to them that I couldn't put into words—a flat, dull quality, like unpolished metal.

Also, I could smell them.

I recognized the smell as that of blood, but it appealed to me now more than the smell of blood ever had before. It smelled ripe, like the best fruit I'd ever eaten.

I'm a full vampire.

Of course. That was the trial, wasn't it? Giorgia had said as much over dinner last night. I'd been told that the simulation would temporarily give me the power and physical traits of a vampire. *That* was what was meant by a physical challenge. This trial was to see how I would comport myself when I'd fully transitioned into my new life.

Well. Easy enough. I just wouldn't eat any of these humans.

And that *was* easy, I was relieved to realize. I had worried over the past months that when I had completed my transition I might turn into a blood-crazed psychopath who would just as soon murder a friend as look at her. But although the people around me smelled appetizing, it was as easy to restrain myself from harming them as it would have been to stop myself from eating somebody else's lunch, even if the lunch had looked delicious.

Was this all there was to the trial? Being around humans and not hurting them?

It couldn't be. This was too easy.

Just as that thought had occurred to me, a hard blow landed between my shoulder blades and sent me sprawling. I landed on my hands and knees on the pavement. Scrambling around, I looked behind me—

And came face to face with a burly man of about thirty years old.

He was bearded, tattooed, and muscled. He was terrifying. I didn't know if he meant to rob me or worse, but I knew a threat when I saw one. I scrambled back against the building behind me, screaming.

He advanced on me.

I screamed again, but nobody around us seemed to notice. Nobody batted an eye. Did no one care that this giant man was about to attack me?

"Please!" I held up my hands. "I don't know who you are, I don't—please don't hurt me!"

He ignored my words and kept moving forward.

It's a simulation. It isn't real. But falling on the pavement had felt real. It had hurt. It *still* hurt—my knees and my palms stung where they had been scraped. If I could be hurt by falling, I could be hurt in other ways, too. I couldn't let this man get his hands on me.

I scrambled to my feet and started to run.

I wasn't a strong runner. I had always finished last when we did the mile in gym class—well, last along with Cecile, who was usually kind enough to run with me so I wouldn't be by myself. My plan as I'd gotten my feet under me had been to run into a store and beg a shopkeeper to call the police for me.

As I began to run, I was taken by surprise all over again.

Running was *easy* now.

The ground seemed to fly by beneath my feet. My ankles, which usually ached with the repeated pounding, felt strong and durable. My feet seemed to fly off the ground with every step.

And I was fast.

I reached the end of the block in record time, rounded the corner, and came face to face with a fire escape. Without thinking, I began to climb. Maybe if I went up, I could lose the man who had been attacking me. Maybe he would think I'd continued straight down the street after turning.

I made it to the top of the roof and paused, looking down on the street below, waiting to see what would happen.

My attacker rounded the corner and without looking up, began to climb.

Okay. So, he must be a vampire too. That was the only thing that made sense. He had followed me by my scent. I scrambled back from the edge of the roof. I had stranded myself by coming up here, I realized. There was nowhere to go. We were going to have to fight.

My attacker reached the rooftop and came at me. I lashed a kick at his midsection without thinking and was stunned when I connected. I hadn't ever thought of hand to hand combat as something I might be capable of.

As the man staggered backward, he tried to catch my ankle and jerk me off balance, but I'd drawn my foot back in too quickly. I spun around, gaining momentum, and kicked him again. Then I lashed out with a hand, jabbing him in the throat.

I was winning.

He hadn't so much as landed a blow, and I'd hit him three times. I had the upper hand. I was going to be able to beat him.

Pride and pleasure at how well I was doing surged through me, and I lashed out with a couple more hits. The man stumbled backward and fell.

"Who *are* you?" he hissed, looking up at me.

"I'm the girl you should never have attacked," I told him, feeling like a badass. On some level, I knew this was all a simulation, that the power I was using to fight this man off had been given to me by an injection, by a serum, and that it was all part of my trials. But was this how the world would be like for me when I'd completed my transition? When I was a full vampire, would I be able to fight like this all the time?

Would I have a reason to fight like this?

I pushed that unsettling question aside as my opponent scrambled to his feet. He was watching me fearfully now, and as I waited for his next attack to come, he turned and sprinted away from me instead.

Across the roof.

Toward the edge.

What the hell was he doing?

I got my answer in a matter of seconds. He reached the edge of the roof and jumped, landing on the next building over. He stopped and turned back to look at me.

The distance was too far for me to jump. I knew that. I could never jump that far.

At least, I couldn't when I was human.

Could I do it now?

It's part of the test, I told myself. *It isn't just about fighting this guy. I have to beat him. That means I have to follow him.*

And that meant I was going to have to make that jump.

Oh, God.

I backed away from the rooftop's edge, took a deep breath, and sprinted toward the edge.

It's just a simulation. But it didn't feel like one. It felt real. The rooftop was real beneath my feet. My hands and knees still stung from falling over earlier. If I missed this jump, if I didn't make it across and fell between the buildings—

There was no more time to think. I reached the edge and leapt.

And then I was flying.

It was a jump like no other I'd made in my life. I shouldn't have been able to go this far in a single leap. I shouldn't have been capable of it. And yet, here I was, sailing through the air. It was miraculous. It was bizarre. It was—

The rooftop of the other building came rushing up to meet me, and I stumbled a bit as I landed. My fingertips went down to help catch me—

My hand curled around a piece of broken pipe.

My opponent had begun to run again, and I could see that he was heading for the far side of the roof, ready to attempt another jump. I chucked the pipe after him and struck him between the shoulder blades, sending him sprawling forward.

And then I was on him.

I hurled myself at his back and knelt on top of him, driving one knee down into his sacrum and holding his shoulders down with my hands. He bucked beneath me, and I knew he should have been able to throw me off. He was bigger than I was. But, to my surprise, I found that he wasn't stronger than me. Maybe he wasn't a vampire. Maybe he was just a human guy. A tough guy, but a human guy.

"What do you want?" I demanded. "Why were you chasing me? Why did you attack me on the sidewalk? I wasn't doing anything to you."

The man just chuckled.

I had the urge to shake him, or to smash his face against the rough stone of the rooftop, but I didn't want unnecessary violence. He had stopped struggling now, so I contented myself with simply holding him down. "Tell me what you want," I insisted.

And then the world around me began to fade to black.

I blinked.

I was back in the palace, looking up at Giorgia, lying in the bed I'd been shown to for my trials.

And Giorgia was smiling at me.

"You did very well, Rena," she said. "You passed the second trial with flying colors."

"Which—" It was hard to talk. I swallowed. "Which part of that was the trial? Fighting that guy? The jump?"

"Both," Giorgia said. "We wanted to see if you could neutralize an opponent. You got extra points for doing it without harming him."

So, I had done well to avoid extra violence. I felt a surge of satisfaction.

"All right," Giorgia said. "You've passed the first and the second trials, and we'll be beginning the third one very shortly. You've done wonderfully so far."

But the third trial was the one I had really been afraid of. I closed my eyes and tried to control my breathing, tried to keep myself calm.

What was going to happen now?

Chapter Ten

"The third trial will be the longest," Giorgia's voice penetrated the darkness. "And it will be the most difficult. But we all have faith in you, Rena. You're going to do wonderfully, we know it."

I was glad to hear that someone was feeling confident, because I wasn't at all. I tried to steady my breathing, to keep from betraying any fear.

"All right," Giorgia said. "Here comes the injection. We'll see you on the other side, Rena."

This time I barely felt the prick of the needle I supposed my system was too flooded with adrenaline to allow me to recognize it. But I knew the trial had begun because I was suddenly sitting in the backseat of a car.

And my parents were in the front.

My parents.

I hadn't seen them since I was a child. Since the day they had died.

I could have stared at them forever, drinking in the sight of their faces.

The fact that I was here to complete a trial seemed to fly right out of my head. What did that matter anymore? Who cared that Cryder was watching, that Giorgia and Samuele were sitting in judgment? Hell, who cared if I went insane and was locked away forever?

Just let me stay here with them. Let me talk to them and hear them tell me they're proud of me.

"Mom?" I said, my voice wavering. "Dad?"

They didn't respond. Could they hear me? The man in the last trial had been able to. What was going on? Had something gone wrong with the serum?

Who cared if it had?

Rain continued to beat down against the car windows. My father, in the driver's seat, steered us slowly along the familiar roads toward the home I had once shared with them. My mother fiddled with the radio knobs, bringing a song into focus, singing along even as she did so.

Now she turned around and grinned at me as she sang. What must she be seeing? She didn't act like a woman whose daughter had suddenly appeared as a teenager. Was she seeing little girl me?

My father joined in the singalong. I had forgotten this, I realized with a pang. I had forgotten how happy they so often were together. I thought of them now only in terms of their relationships to me. I had forgotten how much they loved each other.

It was beautiful to see it now.

I felt more peaceful than I had in years.

What part of this was supposed to be a trial? The only thing I could think of was that I had already failed somehow, and that this was what it was like to be insane. Perhaps my brain was simply showing me images that had nothing to do with reality on a loop now. Maybe I was already institutionalized.

Poor Cryder. He had thought me capable of this. He must be so embarrassed.

It was the thought of Cryder that jerked me back. I had to do better. I had to fight my way through whatever was going on. I didn't know what was expected of me here, but I had to figure it out and face it.

The rain lashed the windshield.

A song came on. A familiar oldie, one that had seemed to live in the back of my mind for years now, one I had never been able to listen to. I always changed the radio station when it came on. I left rooms if someone tried to play it.

A chill ran through me.

This is the song that's playing when they die.

This was the day my parents died.

No sooner had that realization gripped me than my mother let out a scream— "He's there!"

He's there? Who was where? I remembered her screaming. I remembered being jerked out of a daydream. But I didn't remember those words. Who was she talking about? What was happening? Was this what had happened before? It must be, right?

The tires squealed. The car spun out of control.

The air was torn up by screams.

We were rolling—we were upside down—glass was shattering, and my face was wet with tears or blood or rainwater. I couldn't be sure. I didn't know what was going on.

But that was the crash.

That was how they died.

My heart was racing. I felt like I was going to be sick. How dare Giorgia make me go through this again? What did it prove? This was the worst thing that had ever happened to me in my life. How was suffering it twice going to make me a better queen?

I wanted to go home. I wished I had never met any of them.

I undid my seatbelt and dropped from my seat, where I hung suspended like a doll, to the roof of the car below. I hadn't been able to do *that* in real life. I had been only a baby. Everything had been out of my control. But this was a simulation. Nothing could hurt me.

And I was angry.

I would be damned if I was going to stay here in this car with my dead parents the way I had the first time. I didn't need to go through that horror again.

No, I realized suddenly, freezing where I sat.

That wasn't correct.

I couldn't go outside after all.

Because someone was out there.

It tickled at the back of my memory. My mother's scream—

He's there! —I had no memory of that. But I *did* remember some of this next part.

Heavy boots walking around the car.

Pale hands reaching in and closing around my father's arms, pulling him out of the vehicle.

When I'd seen this as a kid, I had thought the police, or the ambulance must have arrived. I had thought the hands were working to save my father. I had been relieved. Because at that point in my life, I hadn't understood that some adults just wanted to hurt you and take things from you.

I had still believed that adults were good people.

I knew better now. I knew *more* now. Adults weren't always good. Adults weren't always even people. Sometimes they were vampires, evil vampires who would cross oceans in search of your blood.

Bristol.

He would never stop haunting me.

Even here, safely locked in a memory that should have nothing to do with him, I was haunted by the very thought of him. I would never be free.

And I knew something else, too. I knew that a man who had recently been through a terrible car accident, who currently lay unconscious, should not be moved as if he were a sack of potatoes. Dragged from the vehicle by his arms.

As I watched the mysterious hands pull my father away, I saw blood trailing from his body, staining the car's interior and the road beyond.

Had that blood always been there? Had that always been a part of this memory? Or had I added it myself?

Why would I have done that?

But I couldn't have just *forgotten* it, could I? That wasn't the same as forgetting the exact words my mother had screamed before the crash. This was my father bleeding out in the rain. I couldn't have forgotten about that.

Unless.

Unless it had just been too horrible to keep in my mind.

Unless I had blocked it out, not wanting to think about it anymore.

And speaking of what my mother had yelled...*he's there*, she had said. But who had she meant?

Could it have been the owner of the mysterious hands?

I had been too shocked when this accident had happened in real life to observe anything. But I was composed now. As difficult as it was to live through all this again, I knew there was no changing what was inevitably going to happen here. My parents were going to die. I was going to live. That was all there was to it.

So, I might as well use the time to try to learn something.

The hands reached into the car again. This part I remembered. *This is the part where they drag my mother out and lay her on the road beside my father. By the time I get out, I'll be expecting to see an ambulance, but I won't. They'll be side by side in the middle of the road.*

But that wasn't what happened.

Instead, the hands opened my mother's door and lifted her out as if she weighed nothing. There was no blood. And as my mother was removed from the car, I saw her shift slightly in the arms of her rescuer.

If indeed he was a rescuer. He looked more like a kidnapper to me.

But more to the point—she was still alive.

My father was dead when he had been removed from the car. That had been clear. But my mother was still alive. And from the looks of things, she was being captured, not killed.

What did that mean?

I remembered what happened next, suddenly and in a flash, as a hand wrapped around my own arm.

I was being pulled from the car.

But it wasn't the same pale hand as I'd seen before, I realized, even as my body thrashed and I tried to resist. I was being rescued from the crash by someone else, someone other than the person who had helped—or hurt—my parents. I was struggling because I had struggled when this had happened in real life and because I was, apparently, powerless to make any changes to these circumstances. But I didn't want to change things.

I just wanted to *see*.

I wanted to see who had pulled my father from the car, and whether they had been responsible for his death.

I wanted to see if my mother was still here, or if she had already gone, vanished, never to be seen again. *How did I ever think she had died in the crash?* Surely someone must have noticed that her body wasn't found.

They must have assumed she was thrown from the car.

They must have assumed her body was in too bad a condition to be identified.

And the decision must have been made not to tell me about it.

But she had *just* been removed from the car. It had happened moments before the hands had reached in to claim me. Which meant that whoever had taken her out must still be around here somewhere.

I could find them. I could finally learn what had happened that day.

But did I really want to know?

After all this time, it felt as though I had finally put it all behind me. I had a new life now, in a new country, with a new family. I was going to marry Cryder. I was going to be a queen.

Maybe that's the trial.

Maybe I can't take my place as queen until I put my past behind me.

The arms closed around me. I was being held in a way that was both familiar and long forgotten—braced against someone's hip, as if I were a very small child. Which, I supposed, I was, in this memory. My body kicked and screamed, aching to get down, wanting to run to my father, who I could see spread out on the road.

My mother was nowhere.

I beat my fists against my rescuer, but he or she only held on tighter. I thought I was sobbing—

I was rising through the mists.

I was back in the bedroom where the trials had begun.

I lay in my bed, in a tangle of wires, trying to understand.

My heart was racing. The mask that had been covering my face hung askew, half on and half off.

I waited for Giorgia to speak, to tell me whether or not I'd passed, but nothing happened.

I looked around.

She wasn't in the room.

I turned my gaze to the window that led to the adjoining room—and froze.

There was no sign of my friends. The only thing I saw was a bloody handprint on the glass.

Chapter Eleven

I didn't know what to think.

I wasn't even *capable* of thought. All I could manage was to hang on to consciousness as the waves of horror crashed over me. *This wasn't supposed to happen. I was supposed to wake up from the third trial and see Giorgia's face. Cryder was supposed to come in and hug me. Cecile was supposed to suggest a party.*

Not *this*.

Was it possible the trial was still going on? Could this be part of it?

That didn't make sense, though. The trial was supposed to make me confront the trauma of my past, not some random traumatic incident that had never happened to me before. This wasn't something in my past. As much as I wanted to believe that I was still unconscious, that this was still part of a controlled experiment, I knew it wasn't true. I was awake. This was real.

God, I couldn't stop staring at that bloody handprint. Whose hand had it been?

Cecile's? If anything had happened to my best friend, it would be my fault. I had been born into this world. She would never be a part of it if it hadn't been for me.

Or had the hand belonged to Cryder? Cryder, the love of my life, who had risked everything to come to America and find me, to save me from Bristol? Had he been harmed now, because of me?

I didn't think I could live with it if he had.

And what if it had been Drake or Samuele? I didn't want either of them to come to harm either. They had been nothing but kind and welcoming to me as I struggled to integrate myself into their world. The last thing I wanted was for them to be hurt.

And where was Giorgia?

I didn't think she would have left me willingly. Not while I was going through that dangerous trial. She wouldn't want me to wake up alone.

Was it possible I had gone insane?

It was my greatest fear. I had been terrified, going into the third trial, that it would be enough to break me. That when I woke up from whatever I faced down there, I would have lost my mind. Was it possible that had happened after all? Maybe Giorgia was here. Maybe all of them were, and I was just hallucinating the terrible sights around me.

But I didn't *feel* insane.

Did crazy people feel like they were crazy? I had no idea, of course. All I knew was that my mind seemed to be working the same way it always had. I felt like I was thinking logically. My thoughts were swirling and panicky, and I couldn't seem to get myself fully under control, but there was an underpinning of logic there all the same.

I would have to work on the assumption that whatever was going on here was actually happening, that the things I was seeing were real. Until I received some evidence to the contrary, that was all I could do.

I sat up carefully and detached the wires that plugged me into the machines around my bed. I was a bit fearful, doing so— what if these wires, these machines, were keeping me alive somehow? But that didn't feel true either. I felt as though my body was working at full capacity. It was just the fear and the paranoia that were holding me back.

Once I had completely unplugged myself, I struggled to my feet. I felt a little lightheaded, but otherwise alright, which surprised me. I knew I had been given drugs as part of the trials. I supposed they had all worn off already.

Still, I would have to proceed with caution. I had no idea what to expect.

I made my way out of the room where the trials had taken place and next door into the observation room. It was empty, as it had appeared. I had to admit, I was slightly relieved by that fact. There were blood stains here and there, and that nauseated me—but at least there were no bodies. That was what I had been most worried about. I had been terrified that I would open the door and see Cryder's lifeless corpse looking back at me.

I couldn't allow myself to become complacent, though, just because he wasn't lying dead in this room. There was the blood to think about.

He could have been moved.

A wave of dizziness overcame me, and I longed to sit down and put my head between my knees. Who could possibly have overpowered Cryder *and* Drake *and* Samuele? And Cecile...she wasn't an experienced fighter or anything, but she was an extra number. And all four of them were gone. What on earth was I going to do if I did manage to catch up with them? If someone had attacked them and gotten the better of them, what chance did I have all by myself?

I had to try. I couldn't just sit back and wait for whoever it was to come back here and find me too. I couldn't allow my friends, my new family, to fall victim to…

To whatever had happened.

I had to go after them. It was just that simple.

I didn't know where to begin, though, and that wasn't simple at all. For lack of any other ideas, I decided to go back to the main part of the castle. It seemed the most obvious place to start. It was the only way out of this little medical area, and once I was there, perhaps I'd be able to pick up some kind of clue that would give me an idea of what to do next.

I didn't like to think about what form that clue was likely to take. More bloodstains? Torn clothing? Or maybe I actually would find their bodies this time. That would be horrific.

God, I thought. *Please let them be okay. Wherever they are, please don't let them be dead.*

I made my way along the corridor that led from the little medical room to the main palace. As I progressed down the hall, I imagined I could hear voices. They sounded like they were yelling. What could be going on? A fight of some kind? Were they raising an alarm?

But *voices* meant *living people*. Somewhere at the end of this tunnel, someone was still alive. And if I could just get to them, I knew I would be able to get some answers. That was all I needed. Answers.

It's not all you need. What if the answer is everyone you love is dead? *What then, Rena?*

No. I wouldn't allow myself to think it. They weren't dead. They couldn't be. Not after everything we had all been through together. We were tied to each other, and as long as I was alive, they must be too.

What could have happened? I didn't understand it. This city was supposed to be such a safe place. Only vampires could reside here. What reason would vampires have to attack each other?

Then I thought of Bristol, of the fight I'd seen between him and Cryder back home, and my blood chilled. Of course, vampires fought each other, and their fights were violent and terrible. I tried not to imagine horrible things being done to Cryder. I kept my mind tightly focused on the path I needed to take and on what I would do when I reached the palace proper.

I paused along the way and listened to the voices, struggling to make out the words. I couldn't seem to do it. I had no idea what was being said. The only thing I knew for certain was that the speakers were unfamiliar to me. They were male voices, but they didn't belong to Cryder. I would have recognized him anywhere. Samuele had a deep, booming voice that couldn't possibly be missed. And Drake rasped when he spoke.

No, it was none of them.

And there were no women speaking at all. Which meant no

Giorgia, and no Cecile.

Of course, it was possible they were just keeping quiet. That was nothing to fear, surely.

But there were other possibilities as well. More sinister ones. And I didn't know what to do about that.

Standing still wasn't going to help, though, and I forced myself to keep moving.

When I reached the door at the end of the hall, I hesitated again. What would I see when I opened it? And more to the point, who would see *me*? It was a frightening thought—but I couldn't allow myself to become paralyzed by fear. I turned the knob slowly and cracked the door open.

And gasped.

The foyer had turned into a war zone.

Fortunately, the war itself seemed to be over. But the place was strewn with bodies. Corpses. Horrified, I sank to my knees. My muscles felt as if they were turning to water.

Not everyone was dead. I forced my mind to focus on that fact. The palace guards—some of them, at least—seemed to be alright. They were shifting the bodies, moving them into piles, then helping to carry them out of the palace. I couldn't imagine where they were taking them. Out onto the lawn?

Maybe I didn't want to think about where they were taking them, now that I considered it.

I did my best not to look at the faces of the people strewn around the foyer, mostly because I was so afraid I would see someone I recognized. If I saw Cryder or Cecile lying there among the pile of bodies, I was going to start screaming. So far, no one had seen me, and I wanted things to stay that way. I was hanging onto my composure with my fingernails.

But without meaning to, without wanting to, I did see one face.

It was a face I knew.

And I could have sworn I felt my heart stop for a brief moment.

The man was someone I'd met in town, when we'd gone for

our tour. Had that been only yesterday? God.

He had shaken my hand, I remembered. He had told me he thought I would make a fine queen, and he was looking forward to serving under me. He had mentioned that he had always been a supporter of Cryder's.

I liked him, I thought. *He took the time to be kind to me on a day when everything was new and strange. That made all the difference in the world.*

And now he was dead. Dead in the foyer of the palace that would be mine.

I should have spoken to him more. I should have spent more time with him. If I had known—if either of us had known—that yesterday would be his last full day on Earth—

I took a deep breath and tried to steady myself. What had happened here wasn't my fault, even though it felt like my stomach was sinking into my shoes. The only thing I could do now was to try to get my somersaulting emotions under control and figure out what had happened.

Maybe there was still a way I could help.

And I had to begin by tracking down my friends.

I closed my eyes, counted to three, then opened them and forced myself to look at the people on the floor. Were any of them young? Did any have Cecile's long, flowing hair, or Cryder's broad shoulders? Was the queen among them? I looked from face to face, my entire body shaking as I confronted death after death, over and over again.

None of the faces were familiar.

I let out a slow breath, even though I knew I wasn't out of the woods yet. The guards were carrying bodies outside. That meant there were more, more than I had seen. Cryder, Cecile, and the rest of my friends could still be among them.

I waited until everyone was looking away, then crept out and eased the door closed behind me. The battle, or whatever had happened here, was clearly long over, but I didn't want to be seen. I didn't want anyone to know I was here until I had gathered some answers of my own.

For example: What could have caused such massive death on this kind of scale? Ordinarily, the doors of the palace were open to outside visitors, but it was uncommon for the foyer to be this full of them—at least, based on the time I had spent here. What was everyone doing here? Had there been some kind of event that they had come to see?

The only event that I could think of, that I knew about, was my own trials. Was that something that would draw a lot of guests to the palace? Perhaps they were here to greet me, to congratulate me if I were to pass or to console Cryder if I were to fail.

If that were true, didn't it mean it was my fault everyone was dead? It was my fault they had all been gathered in one place. It was my fault they had presented such an easy target. I hadn't been the one to kill anybody, of course, but if they were here because of me then I bore some responsibility for what had happened.

If those assumptions were true, then I definitely didn't want anybody to see me yet. There would be questions, questions I didn't know the answers to.

I hurried across the foyer before anyone could notice me and hid myself behind a marble column. From there, I watched as the guards continued their work, moving as emotionlessly as if they had been carting luggage rather than corpses through the front doors.

What could have happened to cause all these people to die without harming the guards?

And if the guards still lived, what did that mean for my friends?

I knew their primary job was to ensure the safety of the royal family. The fact that they were here, doing this work, must mean the royal family was secure—right?

Or did it just mean that the royal family was beyond protecting? That they were already dead, leaving nothing for the guards to guard?

My head was spinning. I longed to sit down, even to allow myself to pass out. Giving in to unconsciousness would have been a welcome relief. But I couldn't do it. I pinched the sensitive skin of my inner wrist, forcing my head to clear. I needed to stay alert and ready for action. I needed to be prepared for whatever happened next.

I heard a small, delicate sound from behind me.

The sound of a throat being cleared inquisitively.

I almost jumped out of my skin. I spun around, heart in my throat, sure I was about to see Cryder standing behind me.

But it wasn't Cryder. It was a woman I had never seen before in my life.

Chapter Twelve

She was beautiful, and she was terrible.

She had long, dark hair that flowed past her shoulders and moved in a way that was almost liquid when she turned her head. Her nose was narrow and small. Her jaw jutted in a way that was somehow both appealing and aggressive.

But her eyes.

Her eyes were red. So bright as to be almost luminescent. I thought for a moment, half-crazed, that if you had turned off all the lights in the palace, her eyes would have shone in the dark.

Her chin was red with wet blood.

As I stared at her, a drop coalesced and landed on the floor.

"Well," she said quietly. "You've arrived earlier than expected."

My mind struggled to make sense of the declaration. "Expected?" I managed.

"You're the queen to be, are you not?" There was mockery in the words. It felt like she saw me as nothing more than a little girl trying on a crown that was too big for me.

Which, if I was honest, was exactly how I had been feeling.

Still— "Who are you?"

The woman laughed. "I assumed you would be back there longer," she said. "Or that you would not come out at all, that is. I won't deny I had my hopes! The third trial has claimed better women than you, Rena Vesten."

She knew my name. Well, perhaps that was no surprise. Everyone here seemed to know who I was. I was a famous face. I was going to be the queen.

And suddenly I understood who she was, too.

The wild eyes. The blood on her face. The death and destruction all around. Surely, there was only one person who could have caused these things. There was only one person who *would* have caused these things.

But how had she come to be here? She was supposed to be locked away for her own safety.

Or for the safety of others, I thought, suddenly chilled. That hadn't occurred to me when Cryder had told me her story. I had never thought she might be dangerous. I had only thought how sad it was, what had happened to her.

It was a shocking oversight on my part.

"You're Cryder's aunt," I said. "Aren't you? You're the queen's sister."

The woman raised her eyebrows. "My fame precedes me, then?"

"Cryder told me about you." I wondered if it was a mistake to engage with her. But then again, talking to her was definitely safer than anything else she might have wanted to do with me. "He told me you took the trials years ago."

"*Did* he?" To my surprise, she sounded delighted. "What a story to tell his poor, innocent girlfriend, about to sit through the trials herself! That couldn't have made you feel very confident about the process." She touched a finger to her chin, seeming not even to notice the blood there. "But perhaps he didn't want you to feel confident," she said. "Perhaps he wanted to see you fail."

"Cryder would never sabotage me," I said. "He would never do anything to hurt me."

"Is that what you think?" she asked "You think you're loved? You think the royal family cares for you, wants what's best for you? Poor, silly little girl. They don't care about you. They don't care about anyone."

"They do care," I insisted, feeling like I was about to go to pieces. "They wanted me to do well in the trials…"

"Of course, that's what they said," she said, her eyes narrowing. "They said the same to me. My sister sat there while I went through the trials. She kissed my forehead before I went under and said *Moira, I hope you do well.*"

"Maybe she meant it," I said. "Giorgia is kind. She's a good queen. She would never wish anyone harm."

"She wanted to be queen," Moira said. "That's all she cared about. It didn't matter to her if I lived or died, so long as I didn't succeed in my ambition to rule. And you, little girl—they don't care what happens to you. They want to use you. That's all it is. They want you to fill the role they think you should have in their kingdom. But your happiness? Your wellbeing? They don't care for those things. Not an ounce."

"You're wrong." But did I know that for sure? I wanted to say that I knew with complete confidence that everyone here at the palace wanted the best for me.

But how sure could I really be of that?

I had only met the king and queen a few days ago. They hardly knew me at all. I didn't think they wished me any particular harm, but of course they had to put a premium on the safety and security of their people. If it came down to what was best for the town or what was best for me, they would choose the town. And I wouldn't even blame them. Any good ruler would prioritize the needs of the many over the needs of one girl.

What about Drake? He wasn't a ruler, and he had been a good friend to me in the time I'd known him. But we weren't exactly close. Drake was much, much older than I was. I was a blip in his life, relatively speaking. How much emotional investment could he really have in me?

Cryder. Cryder loves me.

Yes. Of that I was sure. I couldn't doubt Cryder's love. He had come to America to find me. He had saved my life, more than once.

And there was Cecile. My best friend. My sister. Looking at Moira, taking in her twisted, wicked looking smile and the blood on her face, I knew that the relationship I had with Cecile was one she couldn't possibly understand.

Maybe she and Giorgia had been real sisters once.

But I doubted it. Cecile would never try to steal a throne from me. She wouldn't even take my hairspray without asking first.

I turned my mind from the question and back to the scene of disaster that surrounded me. "You're not supposed to be here," I managed. "Cryder told me. You're supposed to be—"

"Incarcerated? Oh, that's true enough. They tried to lock me away, but I escaped." She smiled again. That smile made the hair on the back of my neck stand up. "I made it back to the palace. This palace is my home too, you know. I grew up here. Just like your precious queen."

"Why did you come back?"

"Why did I come back to my *home*?" Her voice dropped to a snarl. "I have more right to be here than you do, you silly human girl."

"I'm not—" What could I say? I *was* human, wasn't I? I didn't know how much of my humanity remained, but I knew that I didn't have the strength or the speed or the natural immortality that the rest of my friends had. That *Moira* had. I was hopelessly outmatched here. I couldn't hope to win in a fight against her. I wouldn't even be able to hold my own.

The best I could hope for was to keep her distracted, on the off chance Cryder and the others were still alive and were trying to do something that could help the situation. Maybe they were trying to make it to safety. I would sacrifice myself if it meant that they could live. "What have you done?" I asked Moira. "So many dead...It's your doing, isn't it?"

Moira trailed a finger through the blood on her chin as casually as if she were wiping away a bit of chocolate, then sucked her finger clean. I felt like vomiting. "You'll have to forgive my rudeness," she said. "I was hungry."

"Hungry? What do you mean, hungry?" The truth of her

meaning struck me suddenly, with a burst of horror. "You killed them to eat them? That's what happened here?"

Oh my God. Oh, Cryder. Cecile.

I felt my knees begin to buckle and grabbed the column next to me to hold myself upright. It was too much. Too much to take in. This morning, Moira had been nothing but a myth, a cautionary tale to prepare me for the intensity of the trials. I had pitied her, but I had never thought to fear her.

Now she stood before me, and I had never been more frightened in my life. Not even when I had faced Bristol. Back then I hadn't fully understood what I was up against. I hadn't known the full truth about the vampire world and my own place in it. But I knew now what people like Moira were capable of.

And I knew that the blood of a royal—blood like mine— would only make her stronger.

That was why Bristol had been after me. He had wanted my blood for its particular potency.

Oh God. Where is Cryder?

If Moira had really come here to feed on the blood of royals, then Cryder wasn't safe. And neither were his parents.

Neither was I. But I had already accepted that fact. If Moira decided to attack me, there would be nothing I could do to hold her off. I would be dead, probably before I even knew I'd been attacked.

If only I could have somehow maintained the strength I'd had during the second trial, when I'd had to fight that man on the roof of the building. I had felt so sure of myself during that fight. So competent and capable. I had felt as though I could take on anything.

Could I really take on Moira, though? If I had those powers at my disposal?

Something in me thought that maybe I could.

And now a strange feeling was growing within me. From the day I had met Cryder, from the moment I had learned my true nature and purpose, I had understood that I was something between human and vampire. I didn't have the immortality and the strength that my vampire friends had. And yet, I would never be fully human, like my friends at school. Like Cecile's mother, who had been as good as a mother to me.

That had always felt like something to mourn. A great loss.

But now, looking at this wicked woman who had caused so much harm and devastation, who was even now threatening the lives of my friends and family, I *yearned* for power.

I wanted to be strong.

I wanted to be immortal.

I wanted to bring the full might of a vampire queen to bear against her. I wanted her to suffer, to be punished for the things she had done. I wanted to exact a price in blood for the people who had died here.

Moira was smiling at me. "What are you thinking, little human?"

I'm not human.

"You're thinking of trying to fight me, aren't you?" she said, her lips spreading in a grin that displayed her bloody teeth. "You're thinking it might be a good idea to take me on."

I didn't answer. What could I say?

"I wouldn't advise it," she said. "Not unless you wish to die. And I warn you, little human queen, I won't make it quick. It won't be painless. My life hasn't been painless, and I see no reason why yours should be."

My life hasn't been painless. But I couldn't bring myself to say the words. Arguing with Moira might push her over the edge. And whatever she might think, whatever my instincts might be screaming at me right now, I did *not* want this to come to blows. It was a fight I knew I couldn't win.

"You needn't die here," Moira said. She raised a hand to her mouth and picked something from between her teeth. I didn't even want to think about what it might be. "I didn't come here to kill you."

"Then why did you come?" I asked. My voice shook, and I wished I could have spoken with more confidence. I knew she could hear my fear, too, because of the way her smile widened.

"That would be giving away the ending," she said. "You wouldn't want me to do that, would you? It would ruin the surprise."

"I don't like surprises," I managed.

"A shame. I feel surprises are one of the most exciting things in life. Perhaps you're just not looking at it the right way," she suggested, her tone friendly and innocuous now, as if she was just trying to help me out. Maybe she was. She was crazy, after all. It should come as no surprise to see her mood swing wildly from one moment to the next.

"How should I be looking at it?" I asked. *Keep her talking.* I had no idea what else was going on in the palace, where my friends were, what the guards were doing. I had no idea what Moira's plans were. But I knew that as long as she was talking to me, she wasn't hurting anybody else.

Maybe that was the best I could hope for right now.

"You should be looking at it like this," Moira said. "A surprise means you don't know the ending yet. A surprise means it might be better than you hoped."

It might also be a lot worse. But saying so felt like a jinx, like I would be putting ideas into her head. That was the last thing I wanted. "Where is everyone?" I asked. I tried to make the question sound like a demand, like I was already royal, and I was ordering her to give me the information I sought, but instead I just sounded like a terrified little girl.

"Everyone?" she asked. "Everyone is dead. Look around you, little human."

"I don't mean them," I said. "I mean the king and queen. I mean Cryder. My friends. Where are they? What have you done with them?"

She shook her head. "Can't spoil the ending, I'm afraid."

"Tell me if they're alive," I said. I was begging now, and I knew it, but I was beginning to feel insane myself. "Just tell me that. Are they still alive?"

"I know you want answers," Moira said. "Every living being does. But we don't always get what we want, do we? I wanted to rule, and I got a lockup facility instead. You want to know where your friends are, and instead you get to deal with me. It seems unfair, doesn't it?"

"Just tell me what you want," I said. "Just tell me that. What do you want me to do?"

"What makes you think I want anything from you?"

"You've been standing here talking to me since I came out," I said. "You're the one who approached me. You must have wanted something."

She grinned. "You're a clever one. I might have known Cryder would make a wise choice when he selected his queen." She wrapped her arm around my shoulder. I felt like vomiting, but I forced myself not to. "Let's sit and chat, shall we?"

Chapter Thirteen

Moira led me into the throne room.

The moment I realized where we were going, I wanted to struggle away from her. I wanted to break free of the arm that still pinned me to her side. It felt treasonous to be in this room with Moira. Worse than treasonous. It felt blasphemous.

This room belonged to Giorgia and Samuele. This was the room that was being gifted to me and Cryder. I hadn't been here long, but already I could feel the weight and the importance of this place. Already, I could understand what this room meant to the people of La Oscurità.

And I was here with a murderer.

Moira walked across the room as if it were any room in the world, as if she had no understanding of what this place meant to anybody. She strode up to Giorgia's throne—the throne that would one day have been mine—and dropped into it like it was a cheap recliner.

I hated her in that moment.

Before, out in the foyer, I had feared her, and I had felt anger over what she had done to the people in this castle and the people I loved. But that was nothing compared to the anger I felt now.

Before, I had felt *human* anger. Normal anger.

This was something else.

This was wild, pulsing, too big to be contained within my body, and it ripped out of me in a feral snarl that I didn't recognize. A part of me, detached and stunned, wondered if I could have possibly made such a sound.

She regarded me, then let out a soft chuckle. "You're angry, little one."

I was beyond words. I felt my lip curl up, baring my teeth. I was appalled at myself. I was behaving like an animal.

But she's sitting in my chair.

It was more than just that. She was sitting in *Giorgia's* chair. Cryder's mother. She had tried to get there by approved, legal means, and she'd failed, and now she had staged a coup.

She shouldn't be there. She didn't deserve to be there.

I wanted to grab her by the throat—grab her by the throat with my *teeth*—and tear her away from the seat she hadn't earned.

"Hmm," she purred. "I see what Cryder likes about you, girl. You are strong. You are a royal. I'll bet your blood is a real rush." She grinned, bloody lips parting, red-stained teeth showing.

I wasn't afraid of her. Not anymore. I wanted to tear through her.

But how could I be feeling these things? I had never felt like this before in my life. I didn't even know that I had these responses in me, that I was capable of this kind of violent reaction. I didn't recognize myself.

What was *happening*?

But I liked the aggression. It made me feel powerful. It made me feel like I had some measure of control over this situation. It distracted me from the worry at the back of my mind, clamoring for my attention, that something unspeakable had happened to my family.

No. I couldn't allow my mind to go there. I couldn't think about Cryder and Cecile and the rest of them now. I leaned into the anger instead, letting it fuel me. I hoped it showed clearly on my face how close to snapping I was. I hoped Moira was afraid of me.

She should be afraid of me.

That was insanity. Of course, she shouldn't fear me. She had no reason to. She was a vampire, and I was nothing but a weak, fragile, human.

I didn't feel very human at the moment, though.

Moira, for her part, seemed thoroughly unintimidated. She relaxed in her chair and crossed one leg over the other, watching me curiously as if to see what I would do next. As if I was nothing more to her than a mildly interesting television program. "Are you going to attack me?" she asked.

I wanted to. God, how I wanted to.

But it would kill me to do so. She would tear me apart in a heartbeat, and then I really wouldn't ever see Cryder or Cecile again. I couldn't throw my life away like that when there was a chance, they might be alive and waiting for me.

Slowly, bit by bit, I managed to reel myself in. It felt as though I had to consciously force each muscle to relax.

Moria smiled. "There," she said. "That wasn't so hard, was it?"

I cringed at the sound of her voice. Now that my rage had left me, I felt smaller somehow, weaker. More vulnerable. And the way her voice echoed through the throne room did something to me. It was an assault on my ears.

Was this room designed this way on purpose? Were the acoustics in here supposed to make the citizens of La Oscurità feel at a disadvantage? I couldn't imagine Giorgia or Samuele doing something like that...but then, they probably hadn't been the ones to design the palace. And as I looked at Moira, I found I could easily envision a vampire using those kinds of tactics to intimidate her people.

"So, little one," she said. "Are you ready to talk?"

"I can't offer you the throne," I said. "You must know I can't. It isn't even mine yet. I'm not...I don't have the power to do that. I don't think I'm the one you want to be talking to."

"Oh, but you are," Moira said. "You fascinate me. The lost royal, the new queen, returned at last to La Oscurità. And I'm sure your blood is an absolute delicacy."

I thought of Bristol, the cruel and violent vampire who had hunted me back home for a taste of my blood. I remembered how Cryder had assured me that, while others like him would come for me, I would be safe here in La Oscurità.

He had been wrong.

"The blood of the royals really is the finest thing in the world," Moira mused. She wiped at her teeth with her thumb, and it came away bloody. "I can't understand why everyone doesn't want to try it."

"That's because you're insane," I said through gritted teeth.

Moira ignored me. "The *power* it gives you! Especially rogue vampires like me. Separated from the rest, isolated and alone...we *need* power. We waste away, little human. We dwindle to nothing. I need this blood to regain the strength I used to have. And the more I drink, the stronger I become."

"How much…" I swallowed hard. This was the question I had to ask, and the answer I so very badly did not want to know. "How much have you drunk?"

"You'd like to know that, wouldn't you?" she asked, smiling. "How much royal blood has been spilled today…"

I felt like screaming. I reached inside myself for the rage that had protected me when we'd first entered this room, but I couldn't find it. All I could think about was Cecile. My best friend, who didn't belong in this world, who wasn't even a member of the royal family. What good was her blood to Moira?

If she dies for this, I will never, ever forgive myself.

"Don't worry," Moria said. "I haven't had very much yet. Just a taste. Just a little taste of one of them."

"What does that mean? Just a taste?"

"It means they're all still alive," Moira said. "You can drink from a human for quite a while, you know. Blood cells replenish. If you give them time to recover between tastings, you can feed on the same human for weeks before it kills them. And, of course, vampires recover even more quickly."

I thought of one of my friends, my new family members, tied up somewhere, weak with blood loss. The rage ripped to life within me again as if someone had yanked the starter cord on an engine. "Who?" I growled.

"I beg your pardon?"

"Who was it? Who did you put your vile mouth on?" If she said Cecile's name, I was going to tear her apart.

If she said Cryder's name—

No. Don't think about that. God, I was on the verge of losing control of myself already. What was happening to me? I felt so strange, so unlike myself.

How did my brain even have the bandwidth to ask that question while I was worrying over which member of my family Moira had hurt?

What if it was Samuele? Kind, quiet Samuele, who had made me feel welcome from the moment I'd stepped into the palace?

Or what if it was Giorgia? Giorgia was the strength of this place, the backbone, and she had taught me everything I knew about La Oscurità and my responsibilities as new queen. I had been counting on her to guide me through whatever came next.

Or what if it was Drake? He had been so steady and reassuring last year when I'd learned about my true nature. He had been a good friend from the moment I'd met him. I didn't want to see him hurt.

What if I lost whoever it was?

"They heal quickly," Moira said, and once again her tone was musing and distant, as if she wasn't even speaking to me. As if she wasn't even really aware of my presence in the throne room. "They heal quickly, so I really should let them recover. I should try to be patient. Because if I keep them alive, I'll be able to enjoy them for a longer time. That would be wisest. Yes."

Then she smiled sinisterly, and I felt as if my internal organs had turned to water.

"But I'm not Cryder's *wise* aunt, am I, little girl?" she asked. "I'm not the one the family trusts to make good decisions. If I was that, they would have let me rule. They wouldn't have locked me up for daring to try.

"I'm the insane one. I'm the one who does whatever I want,

99

just because I want to, even though it doesn't make any sense."

"You can't," I whispered.

"I can't what?"

"Whatever you're thinking. Don't do it. Don't hurt them."

She laughed. "You have no idea what I'm thinking, do you?"

You're thinking of killing them. I didn't dare say the words out loud. What if I somehow made the unthinkable come true by giving voice to it? What if I was wrong about what she was thinking, and I put the idea into her head?

"They give me so much power," she said quietly. "How can I be expected to resist? How can it possibly be worth waiting for? If I had all that power, if I had all of their blood right now instead of just a *taste*...the things I could do! I would be the most powerful queen in the history of La Oscurità. I would be the most powerful vampire the world has ever seen."

My mind whirled. She was considering killing them, all of them. My whole family. Drinking their blood, right now, for the boost of power it would give her. "You can't," I said wildly.

"You keep saying that," Moira said. "But I can. Of course, I can. Don't you know that I'm in control here? Don't you know that I've got them all locked up, beyond your reach, where they can't hope to get away from me? If I decide I want to, I can go finish them off right now." Her expression was hungry.

"But you shouldn't," I said. My thoughts were racing, and I struggled to keep my wits about me. "You shouldn't use up all your supply at once like that. Yes, you'd be powerful...but it would wear off, wouldn't it? And then everyone would be gone, and you would be left with nothing. The people of La Oscurità would rise up against you."

"They wouldn't."

"They could," I said, not knowing whether I was right, or she was. "And if they did, once the blood wore off, you'd be too weak to fight back."

But she hesitated.

I drew a deep breath. In my old life, my *human* life, deep breathing would have calmed me down. Today, it felt as if the only thing the oxygen was doing was fueling the flames of the anger inside me. Every time I thought I had it under control, it would blaze up.

How dare she sit in the seat that belongs to the queen?
How dare she hurt the people of La Oscurità?
How dare she lock away my family?

When I thought of her sinking her vile teeth into one of them—any one of them—I felt as if I were going to combust. I felt as if my hands might turn into stone. And if they did, I would have been only too happy to put them to work pounding her horrible face.

It was so unlike me to feel these violent urges, to think these violent thoughts. I had never been temperamental as a child. And even as I'd entered my teenage years, I'd been moodier than given to bursts of anger.

Of course, anger was called for in this situation. Anyone would be angry.

But this *rage*? This was new to me. This wasn't something I'd felt before.

I felt murderous.

And suddenly I understood.

This *wasn't* a human feeling.

This was a vampire feeling.

The change that was supposed to happen to me gradually over the next several weeks had taken a giant step forward in the past few hours. Maybe it was the trials. I couldn't be sure. But something about *me* was now fundamentally different.

I would wrestle with the implications later.

For now, all I knew—and all I needed to know—was that I felt *powerful*.

I couldn't be sure, but I thought there was a chance that I *could* hold my own in a fight with Moira. I remembered the way I had fought in the second trial, the way I had surprised myself. Did I have the muscle memory to pull off those moves again here?

"Maybe you're right," Moira said, pulling me out of my thoughts. "Maybe it wouldn't be wise to rush through this."

I felt like I was going to pass out from relief. "You can

always decide later," I suggested.

"I suppose that's true," she agreed. "I don't need that much blood to get started. Just a taste again will do."

I nodded; sure that my legs were going to give out at any second.

"But I'll need more than last time, of course," she said. "This time I'll have to finish one of them."

It took a moment for her meaning to register.

"What?" I gasped. "You're going to kill one of them?" My head spun. Had I pushed her to this?

"There's no need to look so upset!" she trilled. "It's only one! And I'll tell you what, little human. Since you seem so fond of them, I'll do you a special favor. After all, you've been very kind to sit here and talk all this through with me." She got to her feet and glided across the room to stand before me. "I'll let you choose."

"Let me choose...what?"

"The victim, of course." Her wicked smile left me in no doubt about what she meant. "Any member of the royal family you like. Anyone's blood will do. Who's it going to be? The king? The queen? Your boyfriend?"

I bit back a scream.

"It's up to you," she said, and caressed my cheek.

Chapter Fourteen

Her words echoed in my head, on repeat, over and over. *I'll let you choose.*

I *couldn't* choose. There was no way to do it.

I couldn't sentence anyone to die. By saying their name aloud, I would be as good as killing them, and that wasn't something I could live with.

How could I look Cryder in the eye if I gave Moira leave to kill his mother or his father? How could I face the people of La Oscurità if my first act as queen was to murder one of their old rulers? They would think I was as bad as Moira, killing to get to the throne.

I *would* be as bad as Moira.

It didn't matter that I didn't want to do it, that my motivations would be different. That wouldn't make an ounce of difference to the person who died at my command.

She's doing this to torture me.

Of course, she was doing it to torture me. Of course, she was. That much was obvious by the cruel smile on her face.

Any member of the royal family. Well, that had to mean that Cecile was safe, right? She wasn't a royal. She couldn't be chosen.

Except...was that true? It suddenly occurred to me that I had no idea how that sort of thing worked. It was by royal blood and venom that Cecile had been born into her new life as a vampire. Did that make her part of the family now?

Maybe she wasn't safe at all.

Well, Moira couldn't have Cecile. Not my best friend, whose family had taken me in when I'd had no one in the world. I wouldn't be able to bear it.

Nor would I let her touch Cryder. The thought of her harming him made me feel like I was going to explode with rage. If he died, I thought I might tear this palace down piece by piece with my bare hands.

Which left Drake.

Kindhearted, caring Drake.

Drake, who loved Cecile.

Drake, who had saved my life.

No. I couldn't condemn him to death either.

"I'm waiting," Moira trilled.

There was only one way out. The realization settled in my gut like a stone. But at the same time, I felt the panicky fog around my mind clear. I knew what I needed to do. And there was no hesitation, no moral quandary. There was a *right* answer here.

"I can pick anybody?" I asked.

"Any member of the royal family," she said, her eyes narrowing slightly, as if she sensed a trap.

I drew a breath. "Me. I choose me."

Moira's smile widened. "I thought you might," she whispered. "You're so much like my sister. So *noble*. Such a *martyr*."

"Thank you," I whispered, afraid that if I spoke at full volume my voice would shake and betray my terror.

"You think it's a compliment, to be a martyr?"

"I think it's a compliment that you think I'm like Giorgia," I said, and a little more strength came back into my voice. "I couldn't think of any higher praise, actually."

"You haven't known her long," Moira said. "If you had, you would know better."

I didn't answer.

In a flash, she had left the throne and was at my side. I didn't even see her move. I had seen displays of speed and strength from Cryder and Drake before, but never anything to match this. *So, this is what the royal blood does for her. This is what it turns her into.*

The thought was an abstract one. The pain that jerked me out of it was real. She had dragged me back across the room and slammed me into the throne, hard. I felt the warmth of the wood beneath my legs and remembered the last time I'd sat here, posing awkwardly for a picture so Cecile could send a souvenir home to her mother.

She was going to have to tell her mother I had died…

"Last chance, little girl," Moira breathed. "Do you want me to choose someone else? Do you want me to let you go? All you have to do is give me a name, and you can walk away from me right now."

"No," I whispered. I closed my eyes. I didn't want to watch this. Instead, I called a memory of Cryder's face to the forefront of my mind. Let him be the last thing I saw, even if he wasn't really here.

I tried to contain myself at the painful stab of teeth sinking into the flesh of my neck, but I couldn't help it—I cried out with the pain. A moment later I felt the sickening rush of blood being sucked from my body. It was a horrifying and alien sensation.

I gripped the armrests of the throne, trying to force my mind back to Cryder's face. Waiting for death to come.

Then something snapped in my hand.

I couldn't help it. I opened my eyes and glanced down.

A sharp fragment of wood had broken off the throne in my hand.

I didn't think. I didn't question what I was doing. I turned my wrist and jammed my arm forward as hard as I could, burying my makeshift dagger in the flesh of Moira's stomach.

She screamed and staggered backward, and I heard the sound of my own flesh tearing as her teeth ripped away from me. "What did you do!" she shrieked.

I lifted my fingers to touch the wound at the side of my neck, to assess the damage. How badly was I bleeding? Was there a chance I could run away now?

My fingertips came away dry.

I didn't understand. I probed my skin again, but I could find no trace of the wound. Yet I knew—I *knew*—she had been drinking my blood.

It's the serum! The serum they'd given me for the trials had been designed to help me access my vampire side. Of course. I couldn't believe I hadn't realized it sooner. Some of the substance must still be present in my body, and it was accelerating my healing. Thank God.

I looked up at Moira. She stared back at me. Something had changed. There was fear in her eyes now.

I had scared her.

She wrapped her hands around the piece of wood I'd stuck her with and pulled it slowly from her body, crying out in rage and pain as she did so. She threw it to one side, and it clattered to the floor, staining the stone with her blood.

I slid forward, off the throne and onto my feet. I felt my lip curl away from my teeth, baring them. I felt myself sink into a crouch. I did none of it deliberately. I didn't even think about it. My body was acting on instinct.

I didn't even realize, until I saw Moira fall into a crouch that mirrored my own, that these were the actions of a vampire.

I waited for her to spring, but she didn't. She seemed frightened, hesitant. She had misjudged my strength and my abilities, and she knew it now.

Of course, I had no idea where the boundary of my strength lay. But I wasn't going to let her see that.

"Guards!" she shrieked suddenly, the cry echoing through the acoustically resonant throne room. "Guards!"

Two guards were at my side in an instant. They were huge, hulking men, towering over me, and I knew instinctively that I had no chance of fighting them off. Not both of them. It wouldn't matter how much of the serum remained in my blood. I couldn't possibly take them.

One of them grabbed my arm, and I knew right away that I'd

been correct in my assessment. His grip was like a vice.

"Yes, My Lady?" said the second guard.

"Take her down to the cellar with the others," Moira said. Her voice was a volatile hiss. "I thought I could use her. I thought she might help me. But you can't trust anyone besides yourself. I should have known. Put her in a cell until I have further need of her."

"Yes, My Lady," the first guard said.

They dragged me from the throne room. I would have walked under my own power—I had no desire to stay with Moira, and she had mentioned locking me up *with the others*, which had to be a good thing. But the guards seemed to enjoy manhandling me. They pulled me along so quickly that I couldn't get my feet underneath me, even when we reached the stairs that led down into the cellar I had never visited before.

Could there really be jail cells below the palace? Even knowing that that was where I was being taken, it was hard to believe that such a thing could be part of Cryder's home. What need would he have ever had to lock anybody up? I couldn't picture it. He was too kind, too caring. Cryder would never have used these cells.

We reached the bottom of the stairs and rounded a corner, and I saw them.

"Cryder!" I shrieked. I couldn't help myself. I thought my heart might explode with relief at the sight of him. *He's alive. He's okay. Oh, God.*

He looked up at the sound of my voice, and in a flash, he was at the front of his cell, reaching through the bars. I grabbed his hand and pulled myself close to him, feeling as if I was being pulled to shore after having almost drowned. "Rena," he breathed, reaching out to stroke my cheek. "Thank God you're all right. We had no idea what had happened to you. I was so worried."

"So was I." To my horror, I was crying. The shock of it all had caught up to me, and now I clung to him desperately. "I'm so glad you're okay—"

I looked past him. Samuele sat slumped against the wall, his usual regal bearing gone. He has always been pale, but now he looked as white as bone. "He's the one, isn't he?" I breathed. "Your father. She fed on him."

"You know?" Cryder asked. He glanced back over his shoulder. Drake, who was kneeling beside Samuele, looked up and nodded darkly.

"That's enough," one of the guards holding me barked. "Lock her up."

I cried out as they ripped me away from Cryder. "For God's sake!" he yelled, shaking the bars of his cell. "Put her in with me! What difference does it make to you? She's human! She's not going to do anything."

The guards ignored him and led me to a second cell. I could see Cecile inside, curled up in a ball with her head resting on her knees. Giorgia sat beside her, an arm wrapped around her shoulders, watching the proceedings with a cold gaze. In that moment, I realized how dangerous it would be to have Giorgia as an enemy, and I did not envy my guards. When this was all over, she wasn't going to be forgiving.

Assuming we could find a way out of this, that was.

The guards unlocked the cell and pushed me inside. I stumbled and fell to my knees, but that was fine. I wanted to be on the same level as Giorgia and Cecile anyway. I crawled over and sat beside my best friend.

"Cecile?" I asked. "Are you okay? She didn't hurt you, did she?"

Cecile shook her head but didn't speak.

"She's all right," Giorgia said quietly. "I think she might be in shock. She's never seen an attack like this before."

I felt horrible. Poor Cecile. She had never asked to be a part of this life. By rights, she shouldn't even be here. She should be home with her mother, or off enjoying her first steps into the adult world—the *human* adult world. She was a vampire because of her involvement with me, and now those doors were forever closed to her. I wrapped my arms around my friend.

"What about Samuele?" I asked Giorgia. "Is he going to be okay?"

"Yes," she said. "He's already stronger than he was an hour ago. Moira took a lot of blood, and he has some recuperating to do, but he'll heal."

I couldn't imagine how she must be feeling. If it had been Cryder who Moira had hurt, I would have been out of my mind. And for Giorgia's own sister to be the perpetrator of all this violence...I was amazed that she was keeping it together as well as she was.

Pay attention, I told myself. *This is what a queen does.*

"What about you?" Giorgia asked. "We've been so worried about you, Rena. It's your position she wants, after all. We had no idea what she would do to you."

"I let her take some of my blood," I admitted. "Is that going to cause a problem? I thought it wouldn't make things much worse, since she'd clearly already been drinking royal blood."

"You *let* her?" Giorgia asked.

"She said I had to pick someone for her to drink from," I explained. "I couldn't let her choose one of you."

"Oh, Rena…" Giorgia reached around Cecile and pushed my hair back from my neck to reveal my throat, and I could tell she was looking for the bite mark, checking to see how badly I was wounded.

"I'm all right," I said. "She only had me for a few seconds, and then...well, I don't know what happened. The throne broke in my hand and I stabbed her with a piece of wood. She backed off. She looked kind of freaked out, and then she sent me down here."

Giorgia frowned. "Those thrones shouldn't break," she said. "Only a full vampire would be strong enough to break them."

"Well, I think I've got some of the trial scrum in my system still," I said. "My trial ended early, and I've been feeling weird since I came out of it. Kind of ragey and stronger than usual. And then, my bite healed up as soon as Moira was off me. It *was* right here." I pressed two fingers against the spot. "And now it's just gone."

Giorgia gasped.

"What's going on?" Cryder called anxiously from the next cell. "Rena, did I hear you say she bit you?"

"She did, but I'm all right," I assured him. "It's the serum from the trials. It's got me healing up quickly. I think it really freaked her out, actually."

Giorgia shook her head. "It isn't the serum," she said.

"What do you mean?" I asked.

"The serum wouldn't last this long. You've been gone for hours, Rena. It's out of your system now."

"I don't understand, then," I said. "Why am I healing quickly? Why do I feel so...heightened? It can't just be adrenaline."

"It's not," she said quietly. "It's the trials themselves. You passed, Rena. You're coming into your full power as vampire and as queen. That's what you're feeling. It isn't the serum. It's your true nature manifesting." She gave me a small smile. "You're one of us now, for better or worse."

Chapter Fifteen

One of us now. For better or worse.

For better or worse.

I hadn't known what I would feel the day I became a vampire, fully and completely. I had known this was coming, of course, but I had never known exactly what to expect from it. It had always seemed so distant, almost hypothetical. It had seemed like something that would happen to someone else, someone who existed so far in the future that she would no longer really be *me*.

I had thought of it in the same way as I had thought of things like growing old. I'd known, in my human life, that old age lay ahead, but it wasn't connected to who I was in the present.

But that had been foolish. I had known that my vampire life wasn't far away, off in some distant future I could hardly contemplate. It was just around the corner, waiting to catch up with me.

I should have been better prepared.

My mind reeled now at Giorgia's words. *You're one of us now, for better or worse.*

What did that mean?

"Why would it be worse?" I asked her, my voice trembling. "I thought this was a good thing. What's worse about it?"

I realized, suddenly and with a stab of confusion, that Giorgia was backing away from me. She moved slowly, cautiously, and it was clear that she was trying not to alarm me.

She was also positioning herself between me and Cecile.

"What's going on?" I asked, feeling suddenly anxious.

Giorgia inhaled. "There's a ceremony," she said quietly. "It was our plan, always, for you to awake from the trials with Cryder by your side. He should have been right there with you when you first came into your power. It never should have happened this way."

"I don't understand what you mean," I said, frightened. "You're scaring me, Giorgia."

"As a new vampire...you need the blood of your mate," she said. "The blood completes the process, brings you fully into our world. The blood would allow you to ascend the throne."

And Cryder was locked in another cell, away from me. I couldn't get to his blood. "So, I won't be able to be queen?" I asked. It was a blow, but at the same time, it didn't explain why Giorgia was acting so cagey. Did she think I was going to fly into a rage and start attacking people because I couldn't be queen?

Could I blame her if she *did* think that? That was what her sister was currently in the process of doing.

But it isn't the same. I'm not like Moira.

"It's not just that," Giorgia said. "It's..." she hesitated.

"Giorgia. Tell me what's going on." I was surprised at myself, speaking to the queen so bluntly, but she didn't seem to notice my lack of decorum. She was like a cornered animal, so much so that I actually looked over my shoulder to see if perhaps we were being stalked by someone who might mean her harm.

"If you don't get his blood, you won't turn out right," she said, her voice a breathy whisper. "You'll be wrong. Damaged."

Was it my imagination, or did I hear a buzzing sound in my head? "What do you mean?" I implored her again. "When you say *damaged*, what does that mean?"

"She means you'll be like me," a voice said.

I knew who was speaking. I didn't need to look. But it was

as if Moira's voice had placed a hook inside me somehow, jerking me around to face her, throwing me off balance. I physically stumbled as I turned, and she laughed. It was a high, cold, menacing laugh that made me feel as if my insides had turned to ice.

I reached for the righteous anger I had felt before, the desire that had fueled me to escape when she'd had me cornered on the throne, but I couldn't find it. My body seemed to be paralyzed.

"Like you?" I whispered.

I hated to ask her for anything. I hated turning to her for answers. But Giorgia seemed afraid to explain herself, or even to look at me. Moira, for all her horror, was not afraid of me now, and I knew that she was the only one I could rely on to give me the information I so badly needed.

"There are others like me, you know," Moira said. "Other rogues. You don't see us around here because we're outcast from society, because the ruling class—my dear sister and her bleeding-heart little husband over here—they've decided we're not fit to live among their kind."

"You're *not* fit to live among us." I thought that was Drake. The sharp, grating tone was familiar. I wished I could see him. "You deserve to be cast out."

"Really?" Moira cooed. "Are you sure? And is that what you'll say to sweet little Rena when she becomes one of us?" She was suddenly right in front of the bars of my cage, leering in at me as if she was a bratty child and I was a zoo animal. "Did you hear him, little human?" she asked. "Remember those words. Remember what he said when you're thrown out of their society, when you go rogue and become just like me. Your friend here, all the people you love and trust, they think it's no more than what you deserve."

I was shaking. "I'm not human," I told her. "I'm vampire now. And I'll never be like you"

"Oh really? You won't?" she laughed. "You heard my dear sister. You have to drink of the blood of your mate in order to complete your transformation into one of *them*. Fail to do so and you'll be stuck in limbo. You'll be partially turned. That's where rogues come from."

"Cryder?" I asked, trying hard not to sound like I was going to cry. It was a struggle. I didn't think I'd ever been that close to tears, while still managing to hold back, in my entire life.

"It's okay, Rena," Cryder said. "It's all right. This was always the plan. I was always going to give you blood to help you complete the transformation. You and I are soulmates, and all we need is to bind ourselves to each other. Once we do, your transformation will be complete, and you won't have anything else to worry about. You'll ascend the throne, just like we talked about, and we'll put all this behind us."

His words were meant to be reassuring, I knew, but they weren't. I had never felt *less* reassured. Because in that moment, Cryder didn't sound like Cryder at all. He didn't sound like the person who had helped me find safety when Bristol had been hunting me. He didn't sound like the one who had told me his family would accept me, and that I didn't have anything to worry about.

Cryder had always been able to make me feel safe. But now his words weren't helping. He was locked in another cage, and he might as well have been miles away from me. His voice sounded as shaky as mine. I knew he was watching his father bleed. I knew he was terrified.

And then Moira bared her teeth at me. "Sounds nice, doesn't it?" she said. "He shares himself with you, and you live happily ever after. Except—oh, silly me—I put you two in separate cages!" She laughed. "What on earth was I thinking? I can't imagine."

And she gave a little shrug, as if to say that the matter was of no consequence.

It was more than I could take.

The anger I had felt before came roaring back, but this time it was a thousand times stronger. A million times. It felt as if a wild beast was within me, surging forward, fighting for control of my body.

I heard a manic scream.

It took me a moment to realize that the scream was coming from me.

"Rena!" someone was calling my name, but I didn't

recognize the voice. I hardly recognized the word itself as having anything to do with me. My entire world was consumed by the rage. I felt as if I could have slammed my body straight through the bars in front of me, straight to Moira, who was still standing there and laughing as if she'd never seen anything as hilarious as my current situation.

"Rena! Calm down. Try to breathe through it." A hand was on my back. I shook it off. Just the thought of anyone touching me right now was maddening. Everything was maddening. The color of the walls, the pervasive cold in the room—but Moria's screams of laughter were the worst thing of all. I felt my head throb with the sound of them, as if they were coming from inside me somehow.

Maybe they were. They seemed to mingle with my own cries of rage—and now, pain. It was as if something was stabbing me, stabbing me in the mouth. My hands flew to my lips and I dropped to my knees, confused and desperate. As I cradled my aching face, I felt hot blood on my fingers, and something else, something unfamiliar. Something that didn't belong.

Fangs.

I can rip her throat out with these. It was my only thought.

I leapt to my feet, idly licking the blood away from my lips—

From the first swallow, I felt my throat ignite. It was as if my body had been cued, suddenly, to a craving that had been lying dormant.

Blood.

I wanted it.

I ached for it.

More.

"You feel it now, don't you?" A dark voice, a voice I knew I recognized, was speaking. I tried to sift through my memories and put a name to that voice, but I couldn't find it. The need for blood was too all-consuming. I couldn't think about anything else. "You feel the craving," the voice continued. "You feel the price, now, of belonging to the royal family, of being one of them. This is the cost, little human. You may sit on a throne in a fancy palace, but you will feel everything more intensely, always. Did they prepare you for this pain? Did they tell you how it would feel to be one of them?"

"Fight it, Rena!" That voice was near a scream. It was a voice that should have been a comfort, I thought, but how could anything be comforting right now? How could anything be anything besides *pain* and *confusion*?

"You should consider yourself lucky," the first voice said. "You should thank me, little human. You should be grateful. Because I'm not leaving you alone with no way to help yourself, am I? I've given you a perfect way to alleviate the pain you're feeling now."

A way to end this pain? I would take it. Whatever it was, I would accept it gladly, even if it cost me my life. Suddenly, my perspective shifted. This woman, whoever she was, was no enemy. She was a benefactor. She was here to help me. To save me.

I waited desperately for my lifeline to be thrown.

"Yes," she said. "Two delicious little snacks for you. Only one of them of royal blood, I'm afraid, but we mustn't allow ourselves to become spoiled. You must take what you've been offered and be grateful for it."

Grateful. I was grateful. So grateful. I would take anything. *Snacks,* she had said, and when I sniffed, I realized I could smell something. A scent I wasn't familiar with, but an absolutely mouthwatering one. Just the smell of it told me so much. I knew that one taste of whatever it was would soothe the burn in my throat. It would be like finding an oasis in a desert when you were dying of thirst.

It's going to save my life.
I needed it.
I turned.
There were two women staring at me, and I knew instinctively that neither of them was the ominous benefactor who had promised me relief. They were staring at me as if they were frightened.

There was something familiar about both of them…
"Rena," the younger one said. She sounded absolutely

petrified. "Your eyes...they're red. Bright red."

"Stay quiet, Cecile," the older woman said. "No sudden movements. Just stay still."

"What's she going to do?"

"I can fight her, if it comes to that."

She couldn't fight me, though. I knew she couldn't. I couldn't have explained how I knew it, but I did. This woman wouldn't be able to hold a candle to what I could do in a fight. She would be better served by backing down before she got hurt.

I could hear the rush of blood through their veins.

It's going to save my life.

I sank into a crouch and moved in on them.

"Rena." The older woman spoke in a voice that would have been calming if I hadn't been so hyper focused on the sound of her blood. "We're going to get this taken care of. We're going to fix it, I promise you. It's all right. Remember yourself, okay? You're Rena. I'm Giorgia, and this is Cecile. Your best friend. You don't want to hurt her. You love her. It's okay."

I couldn't keep track of what she was saying. It didn't *matter* what she was saying. They were full of blood, rich, delicious blood, and I needed that blood to live. Everything else was irrelevant, and I wasn't going to let their words turn me from my goal.

Closer and closer I stalked them. One of them had her hands up, as if trying to ward me away, and the other was shaking and crying.

And it didn't matter.

I had to feed.

The thought of quenching the excruciating thirst that burned in my throat was hypnotizing. I wouldn't let them get away. Not for anything.

Nothing else mattered

Not the male voice calling my name, sounding as if his heart was being torn apart.

Not the throne I was supposed to claim when this was all over.

Not the people of this strange city who I was supposed to

rule one day.

Vampire or human, it didn't matter. None of it mattered.

I could anticipate how it would feel to sink my new fangs into their flesh. I could imagine the feel of hot blood flowing over my tongue, sliding down my throat, extinguishing my pain. It would be the most sublime experience of my life—of either of my lives, vampire or human.

"Rena," the woman before me whispered. "This isn't you. You know this isn't you. You know who you are. Fight it. Come back to us. You can still be saved. You don't have to be this person. You don't have to give in to violence. We can help you. Let us help you."

I didn't want her help.

I wanted her *blood*.

I bared my teeth and prepared to spring.

ABOUT THE AUTHOR

Tiffany Heiser is the author of Yearn for Blood, the first book in the Blood Origins series. She was born in Killeen, TX. She spent her early years writing and reading, living in fantasy worlds and writing out her feelings in poems.

She grew up with her parents doting on her creative abilities and pushing her to continue doing what she always loved to do. Raised in a small town in Central Texas where she resides ow with her son, their dog, and her son's hamster-along with the plethora of notepads, pens, and books as she continues her dream of writing.